A fictitious account that began with an actual event.

Peter's Quest

A novel by

Don Furr

Published by Nail Prints Press.
Requests for information should be addressed to:
Editorial Director
Nail Prints Press
5975 Airline Rd.
Arlington, TN 38002
Nailprintspress@gmail.com

Library of Congress Control Number: 2025924217
Print ISBN: 978-1-956837-81-0
eBook: 978-1-956837-82-7

Scripture in this book taken from:
The Holy Bible, New International Version®, NIV® Copyright © 1973, 1978, 1984, 2011 Biblica, Inc.™

Cover design: Tori Karnes, Exhibit A, Inc. (www.exhibitainc.com)

Interior design by Zach Zuber, Exhibit-A, Inc.

Printed Globally
For more information visit:
www.donfurr.com

Also by Don Furr

Quest for the Nail Prints

THE QUEST CONTINUES …

Peter's Quest, the second installment in the Quest Series, is the continuing saga by Don Furr that first began with **Quest for the Nail Prints**, a story of three unlikely strangers who come to the realization that they have been chosen by God for an amazing adventure, one so astonishing that even they have a difficult time believing it is real. As the final chapter draws to a close, we find our time travelers have returned to the future, but not without coming to terms with how they have been wondrously and miraculously changed… and even more astonishing, who has followed them into the future!

Prologue
~From the final chapter of Quest for the Nail Prints~

"Come. We have little time to waste!" Peter hurried up the street, frantically searching for somewhere—anywhere to hide. He stopped for a moment and waited as his friends caught up.

"The Master—" He smeared his tears with the back of his hand. "They were so cruel. I cannot believe it. They—they were crucifying him!"

Paul cupped his hand over Peter's shoulder. "I'm so sorry, Peter."

"And they would have killed you too. Those soldiers have been trained to kill, and they are experts at it." Peter drew a deep breath. "Any other time they would have killed the three of you where you stood. But they did not." He searched Paul's face as if he knew the reason for the soldiers' restraint.

Elizabeth's mind reeled. *They could have killed us? I'm not so sure of that. We still have a life in the 21st century don't we?*

"But once they have finished, they will be back for you," Peter continued. "I am certain of this."

As they moved away from Golgotha, the crowds thinned to a few stragglers. It seemed as if everyone was attending the crucifixion. Everyone. Doors to houses were locked. No open windows. No alleys. Nowhere to hide. Up the street, a cripple hobbled along. No help there. They hurried farther still. The professor stifled a cough, clearly out of breath.

Then Elizabeth noticed the movement. A door swung back and forth in the breeze, its hinges chirping with each breath of air. She recognized it; it was their door to the past.

Paul noticed it at the same time. "The well room," he shouted. "In here! Hurry!"

Elizabeth ducked inside, followed closely by Paul and Van Eaton. Peter pulled the door shut and slid the crossbar into place.

Paul scanned the room and weighed their options. There were few. The only things in the room were the clutter of wood and debris still on the floor around the well and a collection of clay jars standing against the back wall, where perhaps one man could hide, but only one.

Kneeling, Paul looked over the well's rim and saw the nails he'd driven into the wall. They were still in place. And the bottom, still littered with the rotted framework, lay just as they had left it, except that it appeared to be dry.

He dropped a stone into the pit to confirm it. *Good.* He worked his way around the rim to the huge nail closest to the top, slid one leg over the edge, and pressed the arch of his foot hard against it. It was solid.

"C'mon guys, let's do it."

Elizabeth and Van automatically followed him over the edge.

When Peter's turn came, he glanced at the door. "Wait. I have an idea."

He looked through the gaps in the door to see if there was anyone in the street. Nothing. He cracked the door open and saw the cripple. He stepped outside.

The cripple hobbled across the street and up to Peter. They

spoke for a moment, then Peter stepped back into the room and locked himself in.

Crossing to the edge of the well, he leaned over and whispered, "My friends, they are coming. I will stay up here."

He scattered rubble to the edge of the well and brushed the footprints from the floor. Then he worked his way across the room to the clay jars and awkwardly crouched behind them.

Outside, muffled voices grew louder as a cluster of men moved up both sides of the street, pushing on every door they came to. Judging from their raised voices, they were mostly Roman soldiers and sympathizers.

As they drew closer, outside the door the cripple's hoarse voice croaked, "Unclean! Unclean!" the sound careening off the walls and echoing through the streets.

The voices grew louder until it sounded as if they were right outside the door. "A leper! I'm not going in there," one man said.

"No one would be fool enough to go there. Let us move on."

As the voices faded away, Peter smiled to himself at the success of his plan.

The cripple Elizabeth had rescued, in fact rescued them.

An odd stillness washed over the room as the minutes passed. Finally Elizabeth reached blindly through the darkness for Paul. He was still there, and Van was huddled next to him.

It had been nearly an hour since the three fled the grisly scene of the crucifixion. Sixty incredible minutes since they'd watched in horror as Jesus' hands and feet were nailed to a wooden cross. But time as they knew it blurred to a conundrum. No longer were there delineations of hours and minutes, but of events. And the events, most certainly orchestrated by God the Father, culminated at the cross.

But there was more—there was most definitely more. Jesus would rise again! As surely as they were there, He would rise again.

It was their precious solace, but now, right now, their fears were tantamount to what had happened. They were fugitives of the Roman Army, hiding like nocturnal creatures in the shadows of despair and sure to be executed if found.

In the quiet of the moment, Paul stared vacantly into the shadows.

"It was even worse than I imagined it would be," he sighed. "I know this is the way it is supposed to be, but dear God, I never dreamed it would be like this."

Van pressed his shoulders against the cold stones that formed the circular pit and gazed up at the opening, tears sliding silently down his cheeks. "I, uh… I don't know quite how to say this." He cleared his throat and struggled to maintain his composure. "But I, uh… I'm sorry. I have lived a lie for so long, more than fifty years I suppose. And now to know the truth, to really know the truth—" He quivered and sobbed openly. "I'm so sorry!"

His words were seamlessly stitched into the fabric of all of their hearts as they huddled close to their new brother. How comforting it felt for Paul to embrace him, to stroke his silver-gray hair, and to share his heartache.

"You know, deep in my heart I always knew I was wrong," Van sobbed. "Even when I argued the point. But something inside would never let me admit it. I guess I just hoped someone would somehow break through."

Paul smiled and squeezed the professor's neck. "Well, leave it to you to go all the way to the source!"

All three laughed collectively and embraced even more. There was deference now—unspoken, but mutually understood. And it was such a wonderful feeling. For they had entered this place as strangers, and now they were family.

Paul pulled back enough to make out the professor's face. Even through the darkness, he caught a glint of Van's tears and a beatific smile.

"I want you both to know…" Van paused long enough to gather

the right words, "that whatever happens, it was all worth it. Even if we don't make it out of here alive, it was worth every minute."

"But there's more," Paul hinted. And for the next hour Van listened as the amazing story unfolded, not once interrupting. And it all made perfect sense. Only where would they go from here? They were on the run from the Roman Army, or at least a small faction of it, and there seemed to be little hope of escape, not to mention that they were 2,000 years from home.

While Paul talked, Elizabeth studied the room. She looked at the nails protruding from the wall like bristles on a brush—single strands of hope that had led them to the Savior and now delivered them from harm's way. She worked one free from the wall and ran her fingers across the cold iron. Her heart fluttered.

"If I hadn't taken those nails…"

"If you hadn't taken those nails, it still would have happened," Paul said. "You know that?"

"I know. But it's… it's so personal now. I really did have a part in crucifying Him."

"We all did."

The gravity of Paul's words weighed equally on each of their hearts.

"But it's not over," Elizabeth said. She straightened, and a surge of courage instantly flooded her soul. "We've got to go back." Her words were determined, but cautious.

Van steadied himself against the wall. "I was hoping somebody would say that."

† † †

Several minutes later, Paul wrestled Elizabeth up and over the top rim of the well. With her help, they repeated the process with Van.

Van grinned when he got to the top. "That was a lot easier than it was the first time."

"You have no idea." Elizabeth laughed. "What do you think happened to Peter?"

Before Van could answer, Paul interrupted, "I don't know, but what's going on here?" He brushed his hand across the door. It was cold.

"What is it?"

Paul turned, but before he had the presence of mind to speak, Van finished his thought. "We're back aren't we?"

Paul felt the hair on his arms prickle. "Yes," he said, with both sadness and hope.

There was an awkward silence as the reality slowly took hold.

Elizabeth cracked open the door far enough to see outside. She squinted through the sunlight and watched children playing on the other side of the street.

"I wonder what day it is."

Van slid his watch to his wrist and illuminated the face. "It's April 5th and according to my watch it's almost 9:30."

Elizabeth pulled out her shattered watch and glanced at the face. It read 10:35, the exact time they crashed through the floor, and the date was the same: April 5.

Paul looked down to see and realized the key was still in the lock. His face paled as he pulled it out.

"We are back. But we're early—"

Elizabeth scratched her head. "I'm confused, how can you be so sure?"

Paul ran his fingers across the jagged notches of the brass key, then slid it into the lock. It turned smoothly.

"When we ducked in here, I broke the key off in the lock. Remember?" Paul glanced across the street again and instantly froze. "Come here! You see the girl? The one with the red scarf?"

Elizabeth looked out. "Yeah."

"That's her." Paul's heart skipped a beat. "That's the girl I saw in the alley. The one the soldiers killed!"

Elizabeth exchanged glances with the professor. "Are you sure?"

"Yes I'm sure!"

There was no mistaking the red scarf, the white cotton dress that fluttered in the breeze, her bronze complexion. It was the woman Paul had seen murdered. He was sure of it.

Van caught Paul's arm and the three turned in unison, their thoughts fusing into one salient point. "Isn't it obvious what's going on here?" he asked.

Paul and Elizabeth waited for the other shoe to drop.

"We can save her. Don't you see it?" asked Van.

"Oh my gosh," said Paul. "For heaven's sake, let's do it!"

Then Van's expression changed. "But you know, we'll never be the same."

Paul slipped his arm around his friend. "You realize that we're already not the same, don't you? And I don't think we're supposed to be."

Van smiled at the possibility, "I ramble like an old man."

"You *are* an old man," Paul smiled.

"I am old like wine. You are old like dirt!"

The time travelers shared a laugh and stepped into the street, fueled with determination, mingled with trepidation as they set out in hopes of stopping a murder.

As they quietly slipped out of sight, the door to the well room creaked open. And Peter peered out.

"With the Lord a day is like a thousand years and a thousand years are like a day."
2 Peter 3:8 NIV

OΠE

The first apostle to set foot on earth in nearly two millennia stepped cautiously into the street. Squinting to guard against the stark sunlight he stole glances in every direction. Each view seemed more peculiar than the last. The tangled web of wires that crisscrossed overhead. The strange garb of the people milling in the street and how many of them spoke to small black boxes pressed to their ears. Mystery and intrigue swept through his imagination. *What kind of magic is this?*

The smells were familiar enough—sweet spices and herbs wafted across the open spaces, but he hardly noticed considering the events of the day. Tendrils of nightmares still snaked through his brain. A rabid mob. A bloodstained cross. The Master's face as the nails pierced His precious flesh. But where was the Master now? His thoughts ran in circles.

Farther up the street, he caught sight of a familiar face, then another. He filtered into the crowd and followed unnoticed, though he should have drawn at least a few wary stares considering his garb. But not-so today, for today is Palm Sunday and the festivities are about to begin.

Elizabeth tugged at Paul's sleeve. "Don't lose her," she whispered.

Paul shook his head in agreement and shouldered his way deeper into the crowd.

A surge of panic battered his brain. He knew the young woman he followed would be dead in less than an hour if he didn't figure out a way to intervene. But how? Or for that matter, would it even happen again? But why else would they have returned to the future an hour before their journey began if not to right such a heinous wrong? The image of the woman's limp body falling to the street flashed through his brain. No, he couldn't take that chance. He had to assume that it would happen again.

Farther back, Professor Van Eaton touched Elizabeth's sleeve. He motioned toward the end of the street as a tour bus rounded the corner and screeched to a halt. "I wonder if we're in there?" he asked. His eyes twinkled as if a child's and a smile spread across his face.

Elizabeth just wagged her head. "I don't even want to think about it," she decided, but she still caught herself watching every window as the bus passed. *True enough, they might have been on that very bus a week ago… or was it today?*

"This whole time travel thing is about to drive me nuts! Could we really have been—"

"Hold on, she's stopped," Paul chimed in.

The three watched as the young woman propped her bike on its kickstand. She straightened her blouse and turned. For a moment she watched Paul curiously as they both held stares, then she turned and disappeared through the storefront.

"Stay here."

Paul stuffed his hands in his pockets and walked casually up the street, scratching his days-old beard as he ambled up to the window.

She was inside. Coolly he walked to the curb and dropped to one knee as if tying his shoelace—a bit awkward considering he wore sandals. He pried a twig from a joint in the concrete and jammed it in the valve stem of her tire. The air hissed out with a whine.

"Excuse me, what are you doing?" Paul stiffened as the young woman stepped through the doorway.

Elizabeth and the professor joined them.

"That's not your bike," Liz jumped in. "What were you thinking?" She helped Paul to his feet. "I'm sorry," she said to the woman, "I'm afraid my friend's a bit confused."

"Perhaps I should call the authorities." It was obvious the woman was well spoken, though clearly perturbed.

"No, please, there's no need for that," Paul pleaded.

The woman glanced at her tire, then Paul. "Well now my tire is flat. What were you doing?"

"I don't know—I guess, I thought this was my bike and I uh—" Lying obviously wasn't one of his strong suits.

"All right, an honest mistake. But what am I going to do now?" The woman seemed more perplexed than aggravated.

Paul exchanged glances with Elizabeth. "Wait a minute." He took the bike by the handlebars and loosened the friction lock. The wheel slipped off easily. "Is that a bicycle shop I see up the street?"

† † †

"That should do it." The man's heavy Israeli dialect was curt, but pleasant.

"You didn't have to buy me a new tire."

"It was the least I could do," Paul said, glancing at his watch. *And the fact that it took half an hour was a good thing, too. If she's here with us, how can she be in the alley with those soldiers?*

In reality, Paul didn't know for sure that what he did was going to change anything at all. *Can an event be changed after it has already occurred, or is it forever trapped in time, destined to repeat itself?* It was a question that haunted them repeatedly over the past week. But the simple fact remained that he saw this woman murdered, and if what they were doing now changed things or not, he had to try.

"My name is Manasseh," She shook Paul's hand. "Are you in the Palm Sunday festivities?"

Paul glanced at his clothes and then the professor's. Both were still dressed in their trappings from the past.

"Why yes we are," Van Eaton said with a wink.

The woman smiled. "I thought so." She nodded with a tilt of her head toward the street. "That must be one of your friends coming this way."

The three turned in unison, their eyes open saucer wide.

"Peter?"

Two

Sunday, April 5

Paul flipped on the light as the four entered the posh hotel suite. The room was so well-ordered, it looked and smelled as if the cleaning crew just left. And it was huge, at least compared to Elizabeth's hotel room, and Van Eaton said his room could fit into Paul's closet. Paul learned early on that Van was a master of hyperbole.

Peter was dumbfounded. Obviously. The walk to the hotel filled his head with so many questions he had no idea where to begin—and the elevator! There were simply no words. He walked to the couch and cautiously sat down, reveling at the softness of the cushion.

Paul heaved a sigh and collected his thoughts. He was happy to be back in his own time, but he was frazzled, his emotions raw. Witnessing the crucifixion only hours before literally twisted his ability to reason with any real certainty. The situation with Manasseh and now Simon Peter somehow managed to follow them back to their own time as well. But how? And why? His thoughts were all over the board.

"Peter—" Paul chortled and stalled. "Where do I begin?"

Peter inspected the room with blank stares, slowly taking it all in. He pursed his lips but couldn't bring himself to speak. Finally, his eyes returned to Paul.

"This should be interesting," Van Eaton muttered. He went behind the bar and filled a glass to the brim. *Tap water never looked so good*, he thought after seven days of living off of the nastiest drinking water he'd ever thought about drinking. He gulped it down and filled the glass again.

Peter watched the three interact as if they were privy to everything that was going on, but he was totally oblivious. And the goings-on over the past hour were nothing short of miraculous, at least from his perspective. And now, the questions inside him were about to explode.

Elizabeth sank to the couch beside the wary disciple, her fit frame hardly denting the cushion. She took him by the hand. "Peter—" she smiled calmly. "What you're going through right now is the same thing we experienced all last week, beginning on this very day." She waited, not really wanting to broach the subject of time travel, which she didn't fully comprehend herself. "I know this is hard for you to believe, but we really do understand what you are going through."

Van Eaton came from behind the bar. "And it was as strange to us then as it probably is to you right now," he admitted.

Peter tried to speak, even moved his lips, but there was no sound.

"Do you remember the night at Solomon's Porch," Paul went on, "when I told you we were from the future?" Peter stared at the picture on the wall, a Monet reproduction, without saying a word.

"Well, it was true Peter. We are from the future… and this—this is the future."

Unwilling to break off his gaze, he finally turned to Paul. "I—I do not understand," he said with a child's innocence. "These are events yet to come?"

The three answered with a collective "Yes."

Peter stood, as if in a daze. He slowly walked to the window and pulled back the drapes, cautiously touching the glass as if it should not be there. "And what of of the Master?" he asked timidly. His breath fogged the glass as he spoke. "They were nailing Him to a cross." He turned as tears slid down his deeply lined face. "What happened to Him?"

Paul could only manage a weak smile. He knew that eventually someone was going to have to tell him the truth, he just didn't want to be the one.

"Peter—" he cleared his throat, visibly stalling. He glanced at Van Eaton who nodded gentle affirmation. "Jesus died on the cross that day—"

Peter's gaze inched up to meet Paul's face. "But it was today," he said, his face taking on an odd expression, as if questioning his own sanity.

Paul slipped his hand over the big fisherman's shoulder and flashed a disarming smile. "Oh my dear friend... you have to understand that this was only the beginning... because three days later, He rose again!"

Peter hesitated, feeling somewhat skeptical for a few moments. "He arose? And where is He now? He is here also?"

Paul gave a side-glance and sighed, but not before Peter read the conclusion in his eyes. He turned and leaned palms down on the windowsill.

"And I denied even knowing Him." Tears spilled from his eyes and plinked on the marble sill. He could almost hear the trill of a cock crowing in the night as the pangs of guilt invaded.

Van Eaton went to Peter at the window. "My friend, I understand your pain," he admitted. "I denied Him for more than fifty years, and yet in those final hours, He forgave me—for everything." He squeezed the nape of Peter's neck as he spoke.

"But what does it all mean?" Peter asked. "Why would the Father allow such an atrocity to His own son?"

Paul paced the length of the sofa and sat down. And for the next hour the three time travelers stitched together the events of the previous week. Incredibly, most of the stories made sense to the big fisherman, and some—well, some not so much, but then again it really didn't matter. Peter knew they were telling the truth, as if the Spirit gave them utterance.

"How long has it been since He—" Peter couldn't even bring himself to say the word.

Paul settled back on the couch and stroked his bristled face. This was the one question he'd dreaded since he realized Peter had come back to the future with them. He took a deep breath and sighed as he let it out. "It—it's been two thousand years Peter."

Peter stood motionless and his face lost all expression. Quietly he sank to the couch and for a moment forgot to breathe.

"The Lord has tarried two thousand years?" The panic in his voice seemed more upsetting than what he actually said.

"A thousand years is as a day—" Paul mumbled. The irony was incredibly thick.

Those were Peter's words from scripture—or they will be. He blinked the thought away.

"But… why am I here?" Peter went on.

"That's the same question we asked ourselves all last week," Elizabeth chimed in.

"But none of us knew until the last day why we were there either."

Peter looked at Elizabeth seeking support. "So, it is your belief that God orchestrated all of this?"

Elizabeth shared smiles with Paul and the professor. "Yes I do—we all do." She answered without hesitation. "I believe it with all my heart. In fact, I believe we might all be a part of it too."

Peter grinned as he tried to process everything that was going on. He considered another time when he followed a man solely by faith and how it was the right choice then as well.

His eyes lingering on Elizabeth, Peter stood and took her by the hand then reached for the professor. Van Eaton cradled Peter's calloused hand in his own and reached for Paul as the four completed the circle. They stood in reflective silence as a sudden and ominous presence swept through each person's being. It was a wellspring of hope.

Glorious. Harmonious. Perfect. Creating a sense of oneness, immeasurable by human standards, but auspiciously present in each of them just the same. *We're all in this together*, Paul thought. *There's no doubt.*

Peter lowered his head and drew a deep, stuttering breath. "*Fath-er,*" his voice broke. "I am overwhelmed with sadness and yet also with hope. Learning of the plans you have made and the mercy of your hand, I stand in awe of your greatness." He stilled as his mind flashed to the cross. He heaved and sobbed gently as the others quietly shared in his grief. "My heart is heavy Father. Jesus was my friend… and yet in your great mercy you have given me a new birth—a living hope through the resurrection of your Son from the dead." Then his countenance brightened. "All praise—all praise and glory to you, the Father of our Lord Jesus Christ… whose abundant wisdom and mercy chose me for this journey. Thank you, Father for these your servants. Thank you for their courage, their commitment—and their kinship."

The three unwittingly tightened their grips as Peter's words sank deep. "We await your bidding."

Three

Sunday, April 5 – Dusk

Paul eased the door shut and walked to the couch. "He's finally asleep." He pulled a throw pillow from the corner of the couch and stuffed it under his arm. "You should have seen his face when he laid on the bed."

"I wonder what's really going through his mind," Elizabeth asked. She picked up the TV remote and studied it. "All of the things we take for granted will be so strange to him—I mean virtually everything."

Van Eaton yawned and smoothed his beard. "Strange? More like mind-boggling. I have a feeling the things we saw last week won't hold a candle to what he'll see here."

"We've just got to make sure that he stays close to us," Paul cautioned. "He needs to understand that he can't be going anywhere without us."

"Agreed."

"But do you really think that God would allow that to happen?" Elizabeth asked almost wishing she hadn't. "I'm sorry, I shouldn't have said that."

"No, it's fine. Honestly, I don't know what God would allow and what He wouldn't. So much has happened this last week that I think anything is possible. But I will say this—I think that it'll be easier this time around."

"What do you mean?"

"Well, for one thing we had to keep our identities to ourselves the entire time, and now obviously we don't."

"Yeah, but what about Peter? We can't tell people who he really is… not that they would believe us anyway." Elizabeth slid onto a bar stool and propped her elbows on the counter. "Sometimes I wonder why God doesn't tell us exactly—" She stopped, recalling the words Jesus Himself had shared with her.

Paul grinned in unison with the young doctor, continuing her thought. "What was it He said?"

Elizabeth cradled her chin in her palm and quoted Jesus' words verbatim. "'Do you not think that the answer was there all along and you just went your own way to find it?'"

Paul nodded in affirmation.

"So, where do we go from here?"

"Well, I don't know how this plays into everything, but I suppose I'll be going on to New Delhi," Van Eaton assumed. "Although it's the last thing I want to do, but it's a good thing too I suppose. I've got to right some wrongs with a few colleagues of mine. But I checked and my flight comes back through here on Saturday."

"And I'm supposed to be at Rashaman Medical Center in a couple of days," Elizabeth added. "Oh boy."

† † †

The subtle drone of the air conditioner was the perfect white noise to lull them all to sleep in various rooms throughout Paul's flat. It seemed like days since they'd slept and they were all at the point of physical and emotional exhaustion—especially Peter. And though questions far exceeded answers, they would have to wait, at least for now.

Looking back over the past twenty-four hours, the four of them spent a long, disturbing night that began at Gethsemane, narrowly escaping a horde of Temple Guards who were most assuredly out for blood. Then there was the Praetorium. Professor Van Eaton watched in secret as the story unfolded. The beatings. The scourging. The blood. So much blood. And the Via Dolorosa. They all watched Jesus drag His cross through the crowds and up Calvary's hill to be crucified. Sleep was hardly a consideration then, but now there was no getting past it.

But even with all of the luxuries the 21st century offered; Peter still ended up on a pallet beside the bed in the master bedroom. Then there were the bathing facilities and of course the toilet. Paul even had to demonstrate to the big fisherman how it worked. Now there was an experience all its own.

In the adjacent bedroom Elizabeth lay sleeping soundly while Paul slept in a recliner in the living room and Van sprawled out on the couch, sleeping more soundly than he had in years and for good reason. The most crucial battle of his life had finally been laid to rest. The Lord Jesus, in His final hours, brought the aged professor into the fold and now glorious peace had taken refuge.

Peter stirred, stretched his whole body and sat up. He smeared the sleep from his eyes and cased the room, wondering if it had all been a dream. He walked to the window and drew back the drapes. The light of the waning afternoon sun pierced the bedroom like a knife, its amber beam exposing the dust that hung in the still air. He gazed out over the city at the modern skyline—the ancient walls and the strange horseless wagons that crept along in endless lines, belching blue vapors of smoke as they snaked along coal black paths that followed the jagged contours of the ancient city walls.

And people—swarms of people moved in both directions, following those same paths.

He wagged his head and inched backward, absently gnawing a fingernail to the quick. Reality was once again taking hold. He eased down to the bed and stared in silence at the mirror on the wall. The Ficus tree perched in the corner. The mahogany credenza. And the telephone atop the nightstand. He lifted the receiver and listened to the dial tone, then replaced it. He combed his fingers through his hair and sighed. He'd acted so calm while the three shared their stories of time travel, taking it all in and outwardly surrendering to the idea that God was in control. But now he was alone and the demons of doubt huddled close, their whispers grating on his conscious. *Is this some sort of foolish dream? I am so riddled with guilt that God could never begin to forgive me. How could I ever be worthy of such a calling as this? Why I denied even knowing—*

He settled against the headboard as hot tears slid down his cheeks and dissolved into his beard. He stuffed a pillow under his neck and in the stillness his chin sank to his chest as he drifted off to sleep.

Four

Monday, April 6 – Before dawn

Peter rolled to his side and stared at the odd red symbols displayed on the box beside the bed, but they made no sense. 5:14, 5:15, 5:16. He shivered as the air from the vent ruffled his cloak and his head pounded—not a new sensation, but it was stronger than usual. He grabbed the TV remote and settled back onto the bed, pressing the buttons as he'd watched Paul do earlier. Moments passed and the screen sprang to life. He squinted at the bright image.

'You can view a list of current movie listings by pressing the star key now,' the voice said.

Peter watched, mesmerized. He marveled at the images and the timbre of the feminine voice that came from the screen. He understood what she was saying, but the letters on screen made no sense to him. Then a phrase caught his attention.

'Capernaum, the Sea of Galilee and the Jordan River are all inclusive on this tour that departs at nine o'clock

every morning from this hotel. Contact the concierge for more details… '

Moments later, the images and voice repeated the information. He watched the commercial again and again, in awe of the message and how it repeated exactly the same every time.

"Capernaum," he sighed. "My home."

† † †

Peter slid on his sandals and cracked open the bedroom door. The living room was dark and cold, the only sounds were those of the cool air whistling past the ceiling vents and Van Eaton's rhythmic breathing. He shuffled across the floor, the carpet masking his footfalls as he made his way to the door and pulled the knob. It stopped with a thud and he froze. Van Eaton's breathing stopped, then returned as Peter gently closed the door and fumbled with the safety chain. He moved quietly into the hallway.

Now what? He glanced in both directions and started down the hallway. Passing the elevator, he studied his distorted reflection in the polished brass doors when a bellman rounded the corner.

"Good morning, sir."

Peter nodded uncertainly, not really knowing how to respond. The bellman pushed the glowing button and the elevator doors eventually parted. Both men stepped inside.

"Floor?" he asked.

Peter's eyes wandered. "Outside?"

The elevator was so smooth that the movement was barely noticeable, but it was still enough to make him uncomfortable. Finally the doors opened and he cautiously walked out.

It was not quite 6 a.m. when Peter slipped past the registration desk and into the hotel lobby. The smell of breakfast foods filled the room and he salivated. His last meal consisted of something Paul called *chips* and a *soda* from the mini-bar the night before.

He belched as he strolled into the cavernous room, across polished marble floors patched with Persian rugs; past hand-carved davenports with crushed velour cushions and floor-to-ceiling tapestries, hung from festooned ornamental supports on the walls.

He inspected the room in awe. In every direction there seemed to be something new, something strange. A grandfather clock, its golden pendulum glistening through cut glass. A grand piano, its ebony finish reflecting every light in the room. And a caretaker, guiding a vacuum over a plush rug and straightening the fringe.

Even at such an early hour, the lobby bustled, mostly with Westerners whose internal clocks were so out of sync that sleep was completely out of the question.

Then there were the business moguls. Power ties and hand-tooled shoes. The Trump types—instantly recognizable, though obviously not to Peter. He moved to a chaise lounge and sat across from two men.

"I am amazed at how much Catholic influence is in this city," one man admitted. "It's everywhere."

"On our first trip over, I noticed the same thing," the other responded. "They seem to have built their churches on all of the historical sights—well, the *Christian ones* anyway."

Peter leaned closer. *Christian?*

The conversation then turned to business and there were some expletives Peter didn't understand. Finally, he stood and stretched. He walked to a tour booth at the lobby entrance and reached for a brochure.

"Do you have tickets?"

Peter turned toward the voice.

"T-i-c-k-e-t-s?"

The man pulled a flashy brochure from a plastic sleeve on the counter.

"For a tour. Bethlehem? Masada? Capernaum?"

Peter's eyes brightened. "Capernaum?"

"Yes, we have a tour of Capernaum, The Sea of Galilee and

the Jordan River that leaves this morning at nine."

Peter knew no more what *nine* meant than how the pictures and voices came from the box in his room, but for curiosity sake, he played along.

"We can charge it to your room if you are staying here at the hotel."

"Yes, he is—" Peter turned to the familiar voice. "And we'll discuss it at breakfast," Paul said smartly. "Thank you."

Paul slid his arm around Peter and guided him toward the restaurant. "You can't be going out without one of us," he cautioned. "This is not the world you came from Peter. People don't have your best interest at heart. Do you understand what I'm trying to say?"

"I believe so," Peter blinked hard. "I am sorry, my friend. So much has occurred over the past day... my mind so filled with wonder."

"I understand, but please don't leave without one of us going with you."

"I will not," he promised. "May I ask another question?"
Paul nodded.

"How long—would be the journey to Capernaum?"
Paul thought for a moment. "A couple of hours, I guess."
Peter scrunched his brow and Paul caught on. "Not very long."
"From Jerusalem, this would have taken *dalet*... uh—" he held up three fingers.
"Three days?" Paul asked.
"Three long days."
"Our times are very different, Peter."
Peter's voice thickened with emotion. "I am so moved by all of this."

Paul took the measure of his tone as he spied a large menu perched atop a polished brass easel. "Are you hungry?"

"I am indeed!" Peter said, studying the menu. "It is so strange... we seem to speak the same language because I understand every word you say, but looking at the words is meaningless."

FIVE

Monday, April 6 – A.M.

Peter had downed three cups of coffee before Elizabeth and the professor had joined them. As Peter eased back into his chair, Elizabeth watched him, recalling the first time he'd tasted the strange brew—from a packet of instant coffee she'd found in her backpack. She wondered if he could taste the difference.

The waiter placed the last dish on the table as the four instinctively joined hands and bowed their heads. Paul lingered for a moment, as if prayer now held a strange new significance. Something that was second nature for most of his life now carried with it a curious new connotation. Perhaps, it was the spiritual side of it, or maybe it was the simple fact that they knew personally the one in whose name they prayed. Or maybe it was all of the above, but whatever the reason, praying was a different matter now.

"Father, thank you for this time together," Paul began. "And for this special time you have given us with our brother Peter—"

The big fisherman smiled with a sweet innocence.

"And Father, thank you for this food we're about to receive and for the hands that prepared it. May it be used for the nourishment of our bodies and our bodies to thy service. We pray these things in Jesus' most precious name, amen."

For a moment, they all sat without saying a word. *In Jesus' name* had never seemed so appropriate, especially for Peter who had in fact, neither used nor heard the term. And yet it was perfect.

"In Jesus' name," he repeated. The four quickly dug in and Peter reached for a bowl of—he didn't know what, but it smelled good.

"May I ask, what does it mean to…" Peter repeated the expletive and they all glared at him with surprise.

"Where did you hear that?"

Peter wiped his chin on his sleeve. "This morning, men were talking."

Van Eaton leaned close to Peter. "That's not a good word." He shook his head. "Not a good word at all."

Peter understood completely.

"By the way, I spoke to the airlines," Van Eaton mentioned. "My flight is still scheduled to leave tomorrow afternoon. Just as it was before—" He stilled for a moment. "It's as if we never left at all."

Paul dabbed his chin. "I know. I wanted to call my wife—it's been a week—at least it has been for me." He glanced at his watch. "But it's one o'clock in the morning in Memphis and I don't think she'd appreciate it if I did. I'll wait till this afternoon."

"Let's get a picture," Elizabeth piped. She came around behind Peter and handed her phone to the waiter who nodded as the four huddled together and smiled. "Cheese."

† † †

Back in the suite, Elizabeth considered the situation at hand. A subtle anxiety tugged at her conscience and it wasn't just her. They all felt it… as if they were all coming to the realization that things would never be the same again.

"I'm sort of at a loss as to what to do," she said, massaging her temples. "I know I'm supposed to be at the Medical Center in the morning, but my heart's really not in it."

Van Eaton slid his hands into his pockets. "I fully understand that. By this time tomorrow I'll be on a plane to New Delhi, but I'd rather not leave either. I just feel like I need to stay here."

"Well, I guess we can slice it any way we want, but the reality is everything is just different now," Paul admitted. "And I don't think it will ever be the same again. Certainly not for me, or you Elizabeth… or Van—"

Van Eaton's eyes met theirs. He was beaming.

"And now, one of the greatest men that ever lived is right here in this room with us!"

They all mirrored smiles, though Peter didn't really know how to respond.

"You don't have to say anything brother," Paul added, squeezing Peter's arm. "It's just going to take some time for you to get acclimated to everything that's going on. Just like we did when we were there in your time. I mean, let's face it, Jesus was literally crucified yesterday," his voice trailing. "And even though we didn't actually see it happen; we know for a fact He was."

Peter's eyes wandered as he reached for a Gideon Bible on the end table and absently thumbed through the pages, not really knowing what it was. He stared at the pages as if they were hieroglyphics.

"Will I return… to, to my own time?" Peter asked with a curious tone. He looked at Paul as if he should know.

"I would think so, just as we did I would think." Paul clasped his hands together, lost in the thought.

"I wondered also, about the young woman we met in the street yesterday— the one called Manasseh. Who was she?"

"You know, actually, she was the reason we ended up back in your time in the first place," Elizabeth admitted. "Kind of makes me wonder what would have happened had she not shown up when she did."

Paul jumped up. "Which reminds me—I still have that tape!" A chill needled his spine.

Six

Monday, April 6 – A.M.

Paul stretched out the cord and located the HDMI plug on the back of the TV. He plugged the camera into the wall receptacle and attached the jacks. The camera beeped and sprang to life.

"So far so good." He pressed a few buttons on the remote and the familiar image washed the screen. In the bottom right corner, the date and time were displayed in block letters. *APR 5, 9:05 a.m.*

"Look at that… that's the front of the hotel." They all gathered around the monitor along with Peter who sat closest to the screen. He sat in awe. In reality, so many strange events occurred lately that nothing was coming as a surprise now. But this? Images of his three friends flashed across the screen. He curiously touched the monitor and settled back on his heels.

"This way Elizabeth," Paul's recorded voice called out. The camera lens panned the plaza, past the crowds to the Wailing Wall. Everything was exactly as they remembered. The camera caught images of Elizabeth's intrigue—and Van Eaton's obvious lack. Even Paul's enthusiasm was apparent from behind the lens.

The camera followed up a long, stone stairway, past a litany of storefronts and tourists that swelled to both sides of the narrow street.

Then, there it was, as if it was a bad dream that had come back to haunt him. The alley. A string of crumpled trashcans lining one side and a grid-work of rusty fire escapes lining the other. The camera lens followed up the disheveled path just as Paul remembered… his heart pounding his chest as he watched the scene unfold—each step bringing him closer to a scene that was burned into his memory. His breathing now was reduced to short, sequential breaths as the lens rounded the corner and then—there was nothing. The camera panned the empty alleyway in both directions and then went blank. The screen washed blue as any unexposed film would do.

Paul pressed rewind—stop—play. Nothing changed.

"I—I don't understand."

A grin slowly captured Elizabeth's face as she came to realize they were becoming part of something bigger than they understood.

"I do—" she conceded. "You did it Paul. What you did today changed it all. You really did!"

For a moment Paul considered the thought. It wasn't so much the act itself, but the enormity of it. The repercussions and of course the consequences.

"But—if I changed it, how did we end up at the bottom of the well… and then back in time?"

Elizabeth stood and arched her back. "Now that I can't answer, but—"

A faint knock interrupted as Paul turned off the set and made his way to the door. He pressed his face to the peephole and sucked in a breath.

"Oh, my gosh."

"What is it?"

He looked at them as if he'd seen a ghost. "It's Manasseh."

Seven

Monday, April 6 – noon

"May I?"

"Please, come in," Paul said.

The woman they knew only as Manasseh stepped into the room. She smiled shyly and moved with a gentle grace, her movements measured and succinct. Her posture was upright, but her eyes cast down in humble respect. She hesitated only for a moment before crossing the room as if sizing them all up, one by one until she came to Peter. The two held stares for a moment as an obscure countenance spread across her face. She moved closer to the lone disciple, then paused and lowered her head. With one fluid motion she sank to her knees and bowed her face at Peter's feet.

"Cephas."

Peter's eyes flashed at the sound of his Hebrew name—the one that Jesus Himself had given him. He drew a long, deep breath and instinctively reached out to her but she recoiled, not actually seeing Peter reach, but knowing just the same.

"Touch me not." Her voice was curt and hollow, reverberating in the room as if more than one voice spoke. Peter stilled instantly.

"My words are for your ears only," she spoke in perfect colloquial Aramaic, but not even Van Eaton understood, though he spoke the language fluently.

Peter struggled to keep his composure, taking in every syllable the woman uttered, but having neither the bravado nor the inclination to respond.

Then, without regard to physics, she appeared almost weightless as she straightened and stood to her feet. Shadows were instantly driven from the room as her face flushed to a ghostly white and her eyes shimmered as if reflecting flames from the pupils to the whites. Smoothly she backed away, her every movement fluid and deliberate as a low resonance enveloped the room, emanating from within her, or so it seemed.

She closed her eyes and lowered her head, allowing her shoulders to slump seemingly farther than humanly possible, all the while the drone increasing, but the tone remained the same—as low as any of them had ever known.

The air transformed into a thick, heavy powder that slowly morphed into a hazy figure. Then from her shoulders, a form majestically unfurled in front of their unbelieving eyes. Wings. Glorious, majestic wings, so lacking in pigment that they absorbed the colors in the room, shimmering like pearl as they rustled.

The room was now washed in a vaporous cloud and a sweet aroma beyond description assaulted their senses. The four instinctively sank to their knees.

The being—now more angelic than human, appeared neither male nor female and had become wholly translucent, only its eyes remaining opaque. Extending its arms upward, its vestment parted, exposing a magnificent crystal sabre that shimmered through an iridescent scabbard suspended from its waist. Ecstasy mingled with fear invaded the room. In all their lives, none of them ever witnessed anything like this.

Towering over them, the seraph stood just shy of the nine-foot ceiling, which was a truly menacing sight for obvious reasons, but there was such an august beauty present that fear turned to perfect peace.

"Cephas." The seraph now extended its hand.

Peter stood with trepidation and inched forward.

"You have come for a very specific purpose," the seraph enlightened. "And just as these three have journeyed to your time, it is now your time."

For a moment Peter forgot to breathe. "But, I do not understand." His eyes pooled with tears, but did not spill.

"Nor did they." The seraph gestured toward the others. "But now, they share perfect understanding."

The three protectively gathered around the apostle. "We are with you," Elizabeth whispered. "And we won't leave you, ever."

"No." The seraph focused on Elizabeth. "You must all fulfill your plans for being here. You are expected at your medical facility, Doctor Stewart. Those plans must not be altered."

Elizabeth winced at the sound of her name, not so much at the admonition, but the utter humility of being addressed at all.

"And my dear professor—you are still expected at your conference. Those plans must not change."

The seraph turned to Paul as if looking right through him. "Pastor Ryann, Cephas will remain in your care for the time. This is how it will be."

Paul's heart fluttered as his tears blurred his vision.

"But, you will all come together again soon," the seraph continued.

Our journey's not over... Paul thought. *Not by a long shot.*

"But how will we know what to do—what to say?" Elizabeth asked.

The seraph smiled, tilting its head to one side affectionately, as if speaking to a child. "As the Father gives you utterance, you will know."

Elizabeth smiled, though she trembled noticeably. The seraph then bowed, the resonance building again.

"Lord most high. We exalt you with praise and honor and glory forever and ever." The seraph spoke as if there were many voices speaking at once. "There is no one like you. You deserve all praise, all honor, all commitment. Bless these your servants oh Lord, in the name of the Father, and of the Son, and the Holy Spirit, all in whose matchless names we pray."

There was a sudden rushing—a warm wind that engulfed the room. And with all eyes shut, they embraced as the wind stirred harder until there was silence and the angel was gone.

EIGHT

Tuesday, April 7 – Morning

Professor Van Eaton stuffed the last of the toiletries into his bag and reached for his inhaler. He thought it funny that he hadn't needed it since he'd returned, but he thought he'd better hang on to it just in case. He dropped it in and pulled the zipper shut. This was the last of three bags. Slipping his arm into his jacket he tugged at his cuffs and focused on the boarding pass on the bed.

Lufthansa Flight 587 to Istanbul connecting to New Delhi was scheduled to depart from Tel Aviv at 11 a.m. He was scheduled to speak at the annual meeting of The United Council of Religious Educators at the Jama Masjid, which was actually located in Old Delhi. This meeting and particularly his speech had been the focal point of his late-night studies over the last several weeks, but now that it was almost here, the meeting held an altogether different allure.

Religious studies were the seasoned professor's bailiwick for as long as he could ever remember—more than fifty years all told. And while choosing such a praiseworthy career had all the earmarks of an honorable vocation, his motives were hardly pure. They may have been better described as a personal vendetta, but against whom? Why God, of course. Yes, it was most certainly God.

It all began with the terminal illness of his mother in the fall of '64. Van was a freshman at Georgetown University when he first received the news. It was a death sentence in those days and it came in the form of ovarian cancer. For five decades, Van Eaton existed in a world of bitter agnosticism. It was a strange dichotomy considering his profession. Religious history was generally considered more of an undertaking for the virtuous, and even the pious, but piety hardly played a part. Then, just two days ago, all of that changed and this contemptuous, crusty agnostic now followed the living Christ with breathless passion.

He glanced around the room one last time. He was leaving Israel—possibly for the last time he feared. He had just spent a most miraculous week—one that to his knowledge had never happened to another human being on the face of the earth, save his two companions. And now the three had forged a relationship that could only be described in a single word. Miraculous. For they began their journey as polar opposites, and now for all practical purposes they were of one mind and most certainly one spirit. And the most amazing part of it all, if *more* amazing was even possible, enter Simon Peter! The apostle himself somehow managed to follow them into their own time and none of them knew exactly how to respond to the situation, if indeed there was a proper way. And then there was the advent of the angel Manasseh. It was as if their journey was starting all over again, only this time with the benefit of being in their own time.

But how could he possibly contribute? A seventy-something college professor whose sole purpose in life had been to refute his Creator. The thought intimidated him to say the least. But the reality was his life was different now. Jesus so wondrously invaded his heart that the only thing that mattered was to serve Him, no matter what the cost. *But am I to negate my obligation to Georgetown when it's been such an integral part of my existence for so many years?*

Isn't living with moral integrity what Christians are supposed to do?

In the quiet of the moment he spied the Gideon Bible on the nightstand. He'd read well into the previous night—overwhelmed particularly with his strange newfound insight and how the imagery of the past week had literally brought the scriptures alive. Now he wanted to share his faith with anyone who would listen and he only hoped that God would see fit to use him.

He wrestled his bags out the door and into the hall, doubting anyone in such a modest hostel could pronounce concierge, much less offer the service.

Nine

Tuesday, April 7 – Morning

"Rashaman Medical Center," Elizabeth pronounced slowly into the receiver.

"Yes Madame, one moment please," the elegantly accented voice responded.

Elizabeth tapped her iPad and read the name. "Dr. Bernstein, please. David Bernstein."

"Speaking."

"Dr. Bernstein, Elizabeth Stewart from the Regional Medical Center in Memphis."

"Ah yes, Dr. Stewart, we've been expecting you. Where are you?"

"I'm still here at my hotel… the Meridian."

"Yes, of course. I'll send a car for you. In a half hour or so?"

"Oh, that would be great."

† † †

Elizabeth pulled a brush through her hair, and for a moment

she held her image in the mirror. Something was different now and it was more than apparent, if for no other reason than the brightness and relaxed look of her face. But it was more than that—more than an expression or emotion. In truth, she knew that it would never be business as usual again. For now there was assurance—a truly blessed assurance that penetrated deep to her very core, dispelling once and for all every rumor her conscience ever dared conjure up. Jesus was real. She had touched His face, His calloused hands. His scruffy beard. She watched Him sleep, watched Him eat and interact with those around Him. And she even watched Him cry out in agony as any human being would when the nails were driven into His precious flesh. But even witnessing such an atrocity was not enough to dispel her newfound assurance! In fact, just the opposite was true, simply because she knew the whole story and it was that knowledge that gave her the strength to endure it. It was an event that completely and permanently congealed her faith.

Oh, blessed assurance. She sought its elusive grasp for as long as she could remember. To know beyond any shadow of doubt that the one in whom she placed her trust was indeed real. Sure, faith had its place. In fact, she knew that it was impossible to please God without it, but the demons of doubt had always persisted—always knowing what thoughts to implant—what temptation to flaunt and specifically which buttons to push. It had been her deepest, darkest secret. But those fears were now wondrously dispelled and from a mire of faithless resolve, blessed assurance had gained an impenetrable hold on her heart.

But what would happen now—now that Simon Peter returned to the present with them? Would she continue to dedicate herself to the profession for which she had so faithfully spent her life preparing? The angel had made it clear that was exactly what she was supposed to do—at least for now. But beyond that, she didn't have a clue, and that was alright too. For she knew unequivocally that God would lead her in the direction He would have her go. There was not a shred of doubt.

Ten

Tuesday, April 7 – Morning

Peter sat across from Paul, squirming in his new attire—Paul's shirt and khaki cargo pants. But the sandals were his own.

Peter was a larger man than Paul across the chest, but his waist was the same. His inseam however was a full five inches less than Paul's. He pulled his leg onto his knee and rolled up his pants leg into a tangled cuff.

"How is it that everyone from your culture understands me—and I them?" Peter asked matter-of-factly. "I can only assume that our languages are different, especially since you are from a different land."

"Elizabeth asked that very question to Jesus Himself," Paul explained as he ran the words through his head again. "'Would our reason for being here make sense without the tools to comprehend?'" Both men grinned at the logic.

Peter stood and paced the length of the room then turned back to Paul. "But what is truly God's plan for me here?"

Paul took the measure of his tone and chose his words carefully. "This last week was life changing for all of us," Paul said after a considerable pause. "For me, for Elizabeth—and certainly the professor." Paul spoke more obliquely than directly to Peter. "But it wasn't until we returned to our own time that we understood the true meaning of our journey. I think it's just going to take some time, Peter."

Even as he spoke, Paul wrestled with the knowledge that Peter himself would die a martyr at the hand of Nero. *Was there no memory of this? And after that? Surely Peter ascended to Heaven and has been there for two thousand years. What of that memory?* But for sanity's sake Paul brushed away the thought. It was just one of those questions he was going to have to let slide.

"There is something I would truly like to do—" Peter took the brochure from the counter and handed it to Paul. "Would it be possible—for us to make the journey to Capernaum?" He raised his eyebrows as he spoke. "To my home?"

Paul took the brochure and glanced at the schedule. "Well, why not? That's a great idea! When in Rome right?"

Peter tilted his head to one side. "*Rome?*"

ELEVEN

Tuesday, April 8 – A.M.

Dr. Bernstein flashed his ID badge at the guard. The chevron-striped gate pivoted open and he and Dr. Stewart drove through.

"This place really is like Fort Knox."

"Excuse me?"

"Oh, it was just something my boss had said when he was trying to talk me into making this trip."

"Ray Roaten?"

"Yes, of course." She looked at Bernstein as if he knew more than he was letting on.

"Ray and I met last year," Bernstein explained. "That's when this whole physician exchange idea came up."

Stewart blinked without saying a word, marveling at how God had orchestrated the perfect scenario. Meeting Paul Ryann on the plane. Professor Van Eaton. Even the Lord Jesus. And now Peter. Never mind the little-known fact that all three were direct descendants of the Magi. It was a secret Jesus Himself shared with Liz and Paul that night in the garden.

A military helicopter whirred in the distance as Bernstein

focused on Elizabeth. "We don't have an air medical unit here, though. I wish we did."

Elizabeth wondered how much Roaten actually shared about her.

"Since we're going to be working closely on this project, would it be okay if we used our Christian names?" he said.

"Of course."

"Do you prefer Elizabeth or Liz?"

"I'm used to being called Betty Lou," she said with a straight face. She could see she caught him off guard.

He hesitated as she jumped in.

"I'm kidding," she said. "Liz is fine."

"So it's gonna be like that huh? Well two can play this game."

Liz blew a raspberry. "I'm not usually so silly, especially in a professional setting—but we've been in such a tense situation for days now, and I guess I just needed to break the pressure."

"If that's the case Dr. Betty Lou, I think I should take you for a cup of coffee before we do business. What do you say?"

"I think that sounds just great Dr. Davey Bernsteen."

They laughed almost hysterically, so relieved to be able to breathe before the serious stuff again.

† † †

"Press that button and push back on the seat."

Peter guided his finger to the steel button on the armrest and pressed it awkwardly. The seat reclined—startling him. He pressed his face against the tinted glass and watched the passing landscape. "I have never imagined such things in all of my life as I have witnessed today. I am so blessed."

Paul settled back in his seat and watched the lone disciple, his hair slicked back and pulled into a ponytail. At first glance it almost made him look like a biker. A few hours of sleep and a change of clothes had really worked wonders on him. A little soap and deodorant hadn't hurt either. Paul grinned at the thought as he watched Peter who marveled at everything from the supple leather seats to the cold air that whistled through the vents overhead. He wondered what God truly had in store for Peter—for all of them in fact. But like Elizabeth, he was resigned to the fact that God was indeed in control.

"To your left is the area where the ancient city of Jericho stood—" the driver chimed in over the sound system. "But as you can tell there is not much to see from this vantage point. There are, however, excavations that are in the works, but the process has slowed since the latest Palestinian uprising on the West Bank…"

"*Palestinian?*" Peter thought. He rarely referred to the name Palestine as the Greeks and Romans had 'branded' their land more than a century before. He wondered if this was still the case.

Paul went on, trying his best to explain the age-old struggle between the Palestinians and the Jews, but it only seemed to muddle the big fisherman's understanding.

"These times are not so different than my own," Peter admitted. "The prejudice of man seems to have changed little, in fact."

Paul considered Peter's perspective as well as his insight. He truly did seem to be adapting well to his surroundings generally speaking, but he knew the journey had only just begun.

TWELVE

Tuesday, April 7 – P.M.

"Leonardo, you old reprobate. When did you get in?"

Professor Van Eaton searched the crowd for the familiar voice.

"Doctor Rosencrantz." The two shook hands heavily. "I landed this afternoon. It's good to see you my friend."

"Well, it's good to see you, too." Rosencrantz seemed intrigued at the salutation. "I figured I'd have found you at the bar."

"I must confess that was the farthest thing from my mind."

"What's that?"

"We need to talk."

"All right… oh, I'd like to introduce you to someone. Professor Van Eaton, Janis Tabor."

The young woman extended her hand. "Janis Tabor—Sun Times." Her eyes sparkled.

Janis Tabor was a plain, unadorned woman on the slender side, more athletic than just skinny. She wore her salt and pepper hair pulled straight back and twisted into a tight bun, obviously for ease and not for style.

"Miss Tabor," Van Eaton repeated. He glanced at Rosencrantz

and waited for the other shoe to drop, which did not. "And what brings you to New Delhi?"

"Why, the conference of course. I've seen you here the past several years professor. We actually met at the conference in Geneva last year."

Van Eaton's gaze fell to the floor.

"It's all right, I know you're a busy man and I understand—a Nobel laureate?"

"Nominee," he corrected.

"Drink sir?" a waiter interrupted.

He scanned the tray. "Perrier will be fine." He turned and Rosencrantz was gone.

"Scotch. Neat," Tabor said.

The two found a tall table and continued their conversation.

"So, how did you know about the nomination? That news wasn't supposed to be out, at least not yet."

Tabor grinned like a conspirator. "Now professor, a good reporter never reveals her source."

Van Eaton crossed his arms and pushed his glasses to the bridge of his nose.

"Besides, it sounds like a good omen to me," she went on. "If I remember correctly, the speech you gave last year caused quite a stir between you and the hierarchy at Georgetown. The *Errant Scriptures*, wasn't it?" She found the narrow straw with her tongue and sipped her spirits glibly.

Van Eaton pulled a handkerchief from his pocket and dabbed his mouth. *That's a genie I can't put back in the bottle, but at some point I know I'm going to have to address it.*

"I'm impressed Ms. Tabor, but quite a few things have transpired since then."

"Oh?"

Van Eaton considered how far he wanted to take the conversation, at least at this point. "Will I see you at the conference tonight?"

She looked up at him through dark lashes. "Oh, I wouldn't miss it for the world."

Thirteen

Tuesday, April 7 – P.M.

"Something's going on here Joe, but I can't quite put my finger on it," Tabor whispered heavily.

Joe Shackle had been Janis' boss at the *Times* just shy of seven years—and not once had he cut her any slack—nor was he about to. "So what is it this time Janis, another conspiracy theory?"

"Joe."

"Come on Janis, you've got to give me something that I can justify spending three thousand dollars for a business class seat just to get you there."

"It's just a hunch at this point, but I trust my instincts."

"Oh great, a hunch."

"Let me ask you a question, Joe. Who was on a plane to Paris the minute the story broke on the Macron thing last month for God's sake? I didn't hear the powers that be complain about sending me there, so how about cutting me a little slack here?"

Silence followed her remark.

"And I just got a tip that he is a Nobel laureate."

"What? Who?"

"Professor Van Eaton. The Georgetown professor, remember?"

"Oh yeah, what about him?"

"Well, it appears that he's up for the Nobel in literature, but he isn't talking about it, which I find rather odd considering the source."

"So, what do you think is going on?"

"I don't know exactly, but I know he's not one to keep that kind of thing to himself."

"What do you want me to do?"

"Well, for starters can you hold the column till in the morning?"

"Jan-is."

"Joe, I'm telling you there's a story here. Maybe bigger than we think. I can feel it. Just give me until tomorrow. Besides, we're twelve hours ahead here. It'll still be morning there when this goes down. Give me until 10 a.m. your time. You can at least do that can't you?"

"Fine, 10 a.m."

FOURTEEN

Tuesday, April 7 – P.M.

"Doctor Stewart, dial extension three-five. Doctor Elizabeth Stewart, three-five."

Elizabeth pulled the receiver from the latch and punched in the numbers.

"Liz. Dave. I enjoyed our dinner last night. Thanks for extending that coffee break."

"Me too. Thanks for the steak. And a great evening. What's up?"

"Can you meet me over in the 'C' wing in fifteen minutes?"

"Yes, of course."

"Come up to the third floor. I'll have a nurse meet you at the elevator and direct you to the BC Unit."

"B.C.?"

"Bio-containment."

There was a pause.

"She'll take you to staging where you'll scrub and be admitted to the ward. I'll meet you inside."

† † †

A duty nurse met Elizabeth as instructed and led her to a set of automated double doors with no glass. She swiped her identification card through the receptor and pressed the paddle on the wall. A series of vent fans sprang to life creating a curtain of air behind her. The door opened far enough for Elizabeth to slip through and closed immediately behind her.

"In here to scrub," Bernstein called out.

Elizabeth rounded the corner and found Bernstein crouching over a long, porcelain sink, his arms lathered to his elbows.

"Just wave your hand in front of the dispenser. It's Hibiclens."

Elizabeth pushed her cuffs up to her forearms. "What's going on?"

"I've got an interesting case I'd like to get your opinion on."

Elizabeth was glad that she and Dr. Bernstein hit it off as well as they had; he an Orthodox Jew and she obviously a Christian, but there was a real connection there. And the fact that he was storybook handsome didn't hurt things either.

She donned a paper gown and walked down the hall, her heels clicking on the polished tile floor as they reached the door.

"The patient in the next room has an interesting malady," Bernstein began. "He's male, who appears to be in his 70's. We don't know for sure. And he's Bedouin."

Elizabeth nodded, grinning.

Bernstein winced. "What?"

"We called them Bedus."

"Yes Bedus. So you know they are nomads, mostly camel and sheepherders. They live in the deserts from Iraq to Saudi Arabia and everywhere in between—here in Israel, Jordan, the Sudan. But they are stateless citizens, so consequently no one nation claims responsibility for them, unlike the illegal alien situation you have going on in America."

Elizabeth took the jab.

"The old fellow in here is a textbook case Bedouin. Plant-diet mostly, goat meat and chicken I suppose. Never had any type of exposure to modern medicine though—antibiotics, sedatives, decongestants. As far as we know, he's never even had an aspirin."

Bernstein looked into Elizabeth's eyes and was momentarily distracted.

"Now understand, there are entire clans of Bedouins out there that are the same way—who've never been treated with any type of modern medicine. Never had their first inoculation for anything… smallpox, diphtheria, tuberculosis, not even the measles. Consequently, these people are highly susceptible to virtually every disease known to man."

Elizabeth's thoughts drifted to Peter. She wondered how his body would react to modern germ warfare, supposing that he would be as susceptible to illness as the Bedus. But then again, she knew who was really in control.

"To Bedouins, something as simple as a sinus infection could turn septic," Bernstein warned. "And something as potent as Covid could be deadly."

"And that's why you have him here?"

"That's why we brought him here initially. But Ali—that's his name. Ali's symptoms are, well, you'll see."

FIFTEEN

Tuesday, April 7 – P.M.

Bernstein tapped on the door and stepped inside. Elizabeth followed.

"Ali, my friend." Ali smiled at the familiar face, though he had no idea what the doctor was saying. "He speaks Najdi, but our interpreter is off today, so we'll just have to wing it. But he's generally receptive to anything we want to do."

Ali's smile stretched into a jagged-toothed grin as Bernstein patted him on his thigh.

"We did a simple CBC as part of a routine work-up and his white cell count was fine, but his red blood cells were virtually non-existent." Bernstein glanced at his chart. "One point two as of an hour ago."

"So, he's anemic."

"Of course, but you wouldn't know it by looking at him, would you?"

"Blood sugar?"

"103."

"Platelets?"

"Platelets are—" Bernstein flipped the page. "Platelets are

normal."

Elizabeth gently took the old man's pulse as he blinked, grinning from ear to ear. He seemed oblivious to the goings on around him, but it was apparent he enjoyed the attention.

"What about his spleen?"

Bernstein's eyes flashed. "That's exactly what I thought," he confessed. "And that's when we made an interesting discovery." His eyes were now fixed on Elizabeth. "He has no spleen."

"But—I thought you said he'd never been treated?" She searched superficially for a scar. "There's no indication of any type of surgery here."

"So you corroborate our findings as well."

Elizabeth looked as if she'd been played. "I—guess so," she said, unconvinced.

"Let's step outside," Bernstein said.

The two doctors walked into the hallway as the door hissed shut. They tore off their gowns and placed them into the bio-container.

"We were going through his things yesterday and made a rather daunting discovery," he hinted.

"What's that?"

"A hazmat suit," he said just above a whisper.

"What? You're kidding."

"No—it was pretty torn up and missing a sleeve, but that's definitely what it was."

"Where do you think it came from?"

"The markings were Iraqi. And it was stamped with the Republican Guard insignia."

"Saddam Hussein?" Elizabeth's voice rose unintentionally.

"Shhhhhh! It appears so."

Elizabeth lowered her voice as an intern brushed past them. "So, you think Ali may have stumbled onto those weapons of mass destruction that 'W' was so adamant about?"

"It's possible—and we found something else in his pocket."

He handed her a plastic bag with a vial inside. "Atropine."

"Atropine? The antidote for Sarin… nerve gas?"

Bernstein seemed surprised at the depth of Elizabeth's knowledge.

"You've been doing your homework, doctor."

"Occupational hazard. Two tours in Iraq," she confessed.

"Well, it appears Ali's been carrying it in his pocket as some sort of good luck charm."

Elizabeth would have laughed if it wasn't so serious.

"And there were traces of Sarin on the suit," he added. "But not enough to pose any threat."

"His isotopes?"

"They're normal, but we took some Bioassays and administered DTPA. We even gave him a prophylactic dose of Prussian Blue, but I really don't think it was necessary."

Elizabeth settled against the wall as visions of Desert Storm darkened her thoughts. "So you think that's why he doesn't have a spleen… that the Sarin somehow contaminated it, and not the other organs?"

"We don't know. We do think he somehow ingested the Atropine though, but we've never had a patient come in contact with nerve gas, so we didn't really know what to think. Then last night we received a call from an American military hospital in Baghdad and they've requested an immediate transfer of Ali to their facility. We're in the process of securing a medical visa for him now." He glanced in both directions. "The hospital seems to be able to turn those things around pretty quick when they need to, but I'm glad they want him there. They can probably do more for him than we can here."

Medical visa? Hmmmm.

Elizabeth considered everything Doctor Bernstein was sharing with her, not fully understanding why this specific situation had come to her attention, but she was sure that God was in it.

Sixteen

Tuesday, April 8 – P.M.

Paul dug through every pocket in his cargo pants until he found his vibrating phone. It was Elizabeth.

"Paul, where are you?"

"Well, you won't believe it, but Peter and I are here in Capernaum."

"Is everything alright?"

"Oh yeah. We got to talking this morning and at the last minute decided to go on a tour, but I can fill you in on it later. Right now we're here at the Sea of Galilee at a cafeteria that serves—get this, Peter's Fish!"

Peter watched as Paul spoke into the device he called an '*I—fone.*'

"I am so jealous."

"I know, right? You can't imagine what today's been like," Paul went on.

"Well, I want to hear all about it. Can we get together tonight?"

"Absolutely, we should be back to the hotel by five-thirty."

"Sounds good. I'll be there no later than six. I've got something

I need to talk to you about too."

Paul pushed the 'end' button and slid the phone back in his pocket, oblivious to probing eyes tracking their every movement.

† † †

Peter and Paul had about half an hour before the tour bus was scheduled to depart. As they left the restaurant they crossed the parking lot to an opening in the copse of date palms that surrounded it. Nearly as far as the eye could see in both directions, the Sea of Galilee filled the picturesque setting. Walking toward water's edge Peter noticed a Bougainvillea—as full and crimson as he'd ever seen. He stopped and plucked a bloom as he gazed out over the vast sea.

"The Galilee is not so very different," he admitted, a bit surprised that it was so. He closed his eyes as the sounds and smells pervaded his senses. The crispness of the air. The wisps of basalt that wafted on the breeze. A sheep bleating in the distance. With long deep breaths he was instantly whisked to another time. He spread his arms wide as if welcoming in the sight, then brought them across his chest. "This—this is who I am—" he said in a soft, but convicted voice. "Or was."

Paul came beside him as the two walked along a riprap-laden jetty that formed a barrier between the open sea and a small flotilla of boats that were moored there. A seagull squawked and another answered as the waters lapped against the rocks where they stood. Peter truly was home, for the moment at least.

"I spent most of my life here," he said. "Along these very banks." He motioned up and down the shoreline. "Even the mud banks and the rocky knolls lining the shores are the same. Oh, the contours have changed and much of the shoreline has a different look it seems, but there is no mistaking it." A smile lit up his face as he took it all in… the sights stirring cherished memories.

Paul listened intently as Peter spoke, his skin prickling the hair on his arms with every word. In the stillness, he pulled out his Bible and flipped through it.

"Can I read something to you Peter?"

The big fisherman nodded gently. "I would like that."

Paul turned to a passage he'd been studying, the pages shivering in the breeze as he pressed them flat. "These are the scriptures I teach from," he said. "And I won't even get into how wonderful and yet strange it is to read with you standing right in front of me, here in this place."

Peter smiled as Paul drew a breath and focused on the text. In truth, it still pained him that he could not read the scriptures for himself, but he knew God meant it for good and that was what truly mattered.

As Paul began, he smoothed the pages as he read.

"'And straightway Jesus constrained his disciples to get into a boat, and to go before him unto the other side. And when he had sent the multitudes away, he went up into a mountain apart to pray and when the evening was come, he was there alone. But the ship was now in the midst of the sea, tossed with waves: for the wind was contrary. And in the fourth watch of the night Jesus went unto them, walking on the sea—'"

Paul looked up at Peter who had begun to sob gently, tears streaming down his weathered cheeks as he turned toward the water. "It says that?"

Paul nodded slowly. "Yes."

Peter pointed toward the line where the sea met the sky. "It was right out there," he said, recalling the scene. "May I share with you the story?" he asked to be polite. Paul was so ready he dropped to the ground immediately, focusing solely on the big fisherman.

"I was hoping you would say that."

Peter gathered his thoughts. Crossing his arms, he paced a few steps, then turned. "We were all on the boat that night—the twelve of us, save the Master," he began. "Jesus told us to go on ahead to the other side of the lake and He would be along." Peter wiped the tears from his face while he spoke. "As I recall it was Thomas who first saw Him, I do not remember for certain, but I will never forget that night as long as I live." Peter sighed and closed his eyes as he recalled the sight.

"He was no more than a ghostly figure at first," he said. "Then finally He came into view and none of us could believe our eyes! It—it was the Master and He was walking toward us there in the midst of the open sea—as perfectly poised as if He stood on dry ground."

He smoothed his beard as he considered the sight.

"Well, we all thought we were seeing a ghost… that is until He called out to us. 'Take courage,'" He said. Peter stifled laugh. "Take courage? How often did we see a man walking on water? It was almost too much to fathom, but somehow He knew we were terrified because He called out. 'It is I,' He spoke in the most calming of voices and it was as if all our fears calmed at once. But then as I always do, I had to take matters further," he admitted as if garnering a fault. "But I had to know that it was truly him, so what did I do?" He looked around to confirm they were alone. "I shouted to Him without even considering the foolishness of the question. 'If it is you Lord, tell me to come to you—'" he said, wagging his head in disbelief as he glared at Paul.

Paul shook his head absently without a thought of interrupting.

"What was that? Pride? Vanity? Some sort of pious belief that I merited an explanation? I mean, what was I thinking? That I was going to walk on the water to Him?" Then his countenance changed and he seemed to look right through Paul. "But that's exactly what I did," he said as if reliving it. "Can you imagine what it was like to step out of the boat and stand on the face of the sea?" Tears again blurred his vision. "It was like nothing I had ever experienced. And then the tempest came—or perhaps it was then I noticed it… and it was so strong one could hardly stand against it on dry ground, not considering that I stood on the waves!"

Paul was so immersed in the story he could almost feel the wind and the spray in his face with Peter's words. In truth, this was one of his favorite biblical events and hearing it from Peter's own perspective brought the story to life, as if he was right there with him. And this was how it was with virtually every story Peter had shared since their journey began.

"I was so scared, I thought I would surely drown!" He plucked a stone from the rocky bank and skipped it across the water.

Paul stood and went to Peter. He put his hand on the big fisherman's shoulder as he went on. "The Master must have thought me an imbecile that night."

"I don't know," Paul whispered paternally. "The way I see it, you were the only one who had faith enough to get out of the boat."

Peter looked quizzically at Paul and whispered a silent thank you. "I—I had never considered that."

Seventeen

Tuesday evening, April 7

Professor Van Eaton cinched up his pants and glanced in the mirror. He was beaming, not so much at the reflection of the man, but the person he had become. Outwardly, he was still the same he surmised; balding and several pounds heavier than he cared to admit, but a little more kempt than before and for good reason. He had a reason to live now… no, he had a *passion* to live and he was determined to be the man God had called him to be. The Apostle Paul had summed it up perfectly in Philippians, a book he'd spent much of the previous night reading. *To live is Christ*, he thought. *No truer words had ever been spoken. Yes, to live IS Christ and he was determined to live what he professed, but he knew it would come at a cost. Perhaps his career, or even more than that, but it really didn't matter. People had to know his heart*, he reasoned. *Those he called friends and those who knew him only as professor.*

He pulled the cummerbund tight across his belly and chortled. *What are these things for anyway?* He tweaked his tie and reached for the door. "Father, the night is yours," he said. "Do with me what you will." He stepped into the hallway and pulled the door shut behind him.

† † †

Elizabeth stared out the window at the waning afternoon sun's amber hue washing the room golden brown.

"It seems odd that the professor isn't here with us."

Paul grabbed the TV remote and pointed it at the screen. "I know, right? I was just starting to get used to the old codger." They both snickered, knowing that Van Eaton would have jumped all over that comment.

Peter twisted the handle to his bedroom door and walked into the living room. Even something as simple as turning a doorknob was such a new experience for him. He marveled at the smoothness of the knob, the mechanism as it slid into the jam and clicked shut. And after locking himself in the bedroom earlier in the day, he knew how to get out if it happened again. He joined them and slid into the recliner, fumbling with the handle that raised the footrest just as he'd seen Paul do earlier.

"Look at you," Elizabeth said. "I can't believe how different you look—so—normal."

Peter rubbed his beard thoughtfully, not really knowing how to respond.

"I mean, you look normal to me. Nice shirt."

"I must admit, the clothing can be rather limiting." He tugged at his collar.

Elizabeth kicked off her shoes and tucked her legs up under her. "So tell me about your day."

"It was something, I have to say—" Paul began. "We started out this morning taking a bus to Capernaum and even the bus ride was an event for our friend here." Paul's eyes flitted to Peter. "Sometimes I forget that virtually everything we think of as normal is definitely not to him."

Peter listened without comment as Paul shared the story with

Elizabeth. They were all beginning to experience a closeness that literally had to forge two millennia, and that is exactly what was happening.

"I never imagined making such a journey could have been as pleasurable as this," Peter admitted. "To sit and be transported in such… such prestige. Only kings should be so privileged. This— what was the word you taught me? Tek—"

"Technology," Paul said.

"Tek-noligy. Yes. It is truly a remarkable thing."

"And you haven't seen anything yet, my friend," said Paul. "I can't wait for you to see an airplane."

"*Air-plain?*"

"It's not important right now."

"Well—it might be more relevant than you think," Elizabeth hinted. She pulled out a large manila envelope and placed it on her lap. "I had a very interesting case today at the medical center," she said. "An elderly Bedouin man that the hospital is transferring to Baghdad. The case is strange enough, which I really can't talk about anyway, but the whole thing brought up a very interesting point." Elizabeth straightened and placed her feet flat on the floor. "I'm supposed to be leaving here in ten days."

"I've been thinking a lot about that myself," Paul sighed.

Elizabeth was now on her feet and beginning to pace. "Well, believe it or not, I think I know what we're supposed to do… or at least our next step anyway."

Paul plugged up the coffee maker and began filling the carafe with water.

"I'm all ears."

"Well, first we're going to have to get Peter a visa," she said matter-of-factly. "And I think I know how to get it."

She pried open the brass clip on the envelope and pulled out a stack of paperwork. "This is an application for a Medical Visa transfer I picked up this afternoon."

Paul pulled off the cover page and skimmed over it. "To the

United States?"

Elizabeth gave a cryptic smile and nodded. "Yep."

"So what are the requirements?"

"Well—basically, a patient has to be diagnosed with an illness or treatable condition."

Paul turned to the second page and glanced up at Elizabeth. "But nothing's wrong with him. Doesn't there have to be a valid reason for a medical visa?"

"Yes, of course." Elizabeth scolded him with an angry glare.

Paul caught the measure of her tone. "I'm sorry. You're trying to tell us what we need to do and I'm trying to throw you under the bus. So what are you thinking?"

Why would he throw Elizabeth under a bus? Peter thought.

"I don't know exactly. I just know that we've somehow got to get a work-up on Peter."

"Then that's how we need to pray."

Elizabeth looked at Peter. "I don't even know if they're going to find anything wrong with him, I just know that he needs to come with me to the medical center tomorrow. And I don't even know how I know that."

"Well, it doesn't matter how you know, the fact is you do and that's good enough for me," said Paul.

Peter joined them at the bar. "And me."

Suddenly the coffee maker belched and steam poured from the top.

Peter already had a cup in his hand.

Eighteen

Tuesday evening, April 7

Professor Van Eaton stood in the shadows, fiddling anxiously with the notes he'd spent half the night preparing. Gently he drew back the curtain and gazed out over the crowd. Tears of compassion welled. So many faces he recognized, but many more he did not. For a moment he wished for anonymity, supposing that what he was about to share would be more easily accepted by those who had never made his acquaintance at all.

He swallowed hard. *How do you share such a life-altering experience with those who have known you at your worst?* he thought. *But then again, the opinions of others are neither controllable, nor are they avoidable,* he reasoned. This had been his typical, textbook reply to his students for as long as he could remember. But typical was hardly applicable now—now that Jesus had gained a stronghold on his heart.

He dropped the curtain and took one last look at his notes. "Father, grant me clarity of mind to do your bidding," he prayed. "Help me to be worthy of my calling, your instrument—your vessel—your messenger, in Jesus most precious name I pray…"

† † †

"Ladies and gentlemen, it is my great pleasure to introduce to you a man who is certainly no stranger to our esteemed assembly," the gruff, baritone voice with a hint of German dialect echoed across the room. "A PhD in divinity and religious sciences, Georgetown University. Master of Arts in Judaic Studies, Biola University… and professor of religious studies at Georgetown University for more than forty years." He glanced behind the curtain at Van Eaton and cleared his throat. "And we just received word, a Nobel nominee."

There was a hush, then a trickling of applause.

"So, without further ado, may I present to you, Professor Leonardo Van Eaton."

Professor Van Eaton walked with effort toward the podium amid a modest ovation. He stroked his forearm as phantom pain needled from his fingers to his elbow… a wound that led to his first encounter with Jesus, and now not so much as a scar remained. He drew a deep, stuttering breath and gazed out over the room. Associates and adversaries alike were sprinkled amongst a sea of faces, all representing the various religions of the world: Protestantism, Catholicism, Judaism, Islam and dozens of factions in between. Clergy from the four corners of the earth; Orthodoxy, Heterodoxy, Monotheism, Polytheism, Pantheism, all represented in their own splendid glory. And there in the midst, Janis Tabor sat poised, her iPad perched on her lap. Unbeknownst to Professor Van Eaton, she held a lethal weapon loaded for big game, and the season just opened.

Van Eaton reached to tweak his hearing aid and grinned, appreciating the fact that it was more muscle memory than anything else. The medications and devices he once was so heavily dependent upon were simply not needed now.

Squinting through the lights, he looked past the facades of black ties and diamond chokers and thus targeted their hearts. But how would he reduce to words the miraculous events of the past week? How could he bring them to understand the depth of sacrifice that Christ truly paid on the cross and all that he'd witnessed? He wasn't sure, but he knew he had to try. He reached for his notes but realized there was no need.

"Ladies and gentlemen—" he began. His words were soft, his timbre as delicate as he'd ever known… as if it was not him speaking at all.

"I address you today with utmost humility." The microphone whined with feedback as the room fell silent, an air of significance quietly spilling in.

"For what I am about to share with you I fear many of you will not accept, either because of your religious affiliation or simply your own cultural indoctrination, though in most cases I have come to learn that the two appear to be inseparable." He glanced over the top of his glasses in an attempt to lighten the air, which sadly he did not.

"Sadly, I must also admit my own shortcomings in that there have been many times over the course of the past week that I myself have wrestled with my own *indoctrination* as well, if you will. But please be assured that I have no doubts as to the validity of what I am about to share with you." He pulled a handkerchief from his pocket and mopped his brow.

"This past week, a truly life-altering event occurred in my life… a life where there has been so strong a spiritual drought that even I am surprised I have let it go on as long as it has. But in fact it has and I have no one to blame but myself. And to be quite honest I still have a hard time believing that such an event actually happened and especially to me, Leonardo Van Eaton—not the most congenial of fellows." Again he paused for effect amid a medley of snickers coursing through the audience. "But as I am standing here, my heart pounding within my chest and every beat reminding me of the significance of the moment, I am absolutely certain of the message I must share."

He pulled his readers from his face and took hold of the lectern by the two front corners, much like a country preacher about to rain fire and brimstone. He struggled for a moment, straining to reduce his thoughts to words, the exact words that God was laying on his heart. Finally he went on. "I've come to understand, as so many of you here in this room, that we, ladies and gentlemen, are biproducts of our own specific cultures, fashioned by generation upon generation of traditions, ethnicities, ideologies… those elements, that have come to define us. But I've come to another realization, one no less significant, and perhaps even more so. That God is neither cultural nor ethnic." His eyes wandered the room for a moment. "Dr. Rajid Guron my dear friend—highly respected servant of the Sikh faith." Guron nodded amid accolades from those around him. "And Professor Stevens, my Mormon brother. You have always been a testament to your faith." Van Eaton paused as empathy swelled in his heart for his dear brother.

"I uh—I spent most of last evening reading from a book to which I claim to be an authority. But I must admit that I have come to learn that the knowledge I possess is superficial at best. Oh, I know what is written on the pages. The verb tenses and so forth, but all of this acquired knowledge is of little consequence if your heart is not a part of it." Tears glistened in his eyes as he spoke. He slid his hand into his breast pocket and pulled out a tattered pocket testament and placed it on the lectern in front of him. Turning to the dog-eared page, he squinted and adjusted his readers.

"The Apostle Paul said: *I consider everything loss compared to the surpassing greatness of knowing Christ Jesus my Lord, for whose sake I have lost all things. I consider them rubbish that I may gain Christ and be found in him, not having a righteousness of my own that comes from the law, but that which is through faith in Christ—the righteousness that comes from God and is by faith.*"

He smoothly folded the book closed with hands that were noticeably shaking. A stray cough cut the air and then another, but otherwise the room was dead silent.

All eyes were fixed on the surly educator; everyone wondering specifically where he was going with all of this. Of course, many in the crowd were dutifully aware of the professor's antics, but it seemed those traits on this particular night were oddly missing, as if a different man stood behind the podium. And even though the assembly as a whole had come to expect the inexorable sarcasm and cynicism, the council members themselves had done little to dissuade him in the past. It was almost as if they fed on the disparagement he typically roused.

The professor adjusted his lapels and edged away from the podium.

"Even when he was bound in chains and confined to a filthy prison cell, the Apostle Paul kept his faith—even celebrating the Lord's work in his life. In fact, he wrote this letter from a prison cell to the Philippians and yet he was *filled* with rejoicing." His eyes sparkled as a smile crept across his face. "Filled!"

The professor now stood erect—manic determination coursing through his veins and powered solely by the promptings of the Spirit. "I stand before you a changed man—a different man from that of years past. A very different man indeed." He studied particular faces in the crowd, hoping they would receive his words. "For I too am filled with rejoicing, just as the Apostle Paul claimed more than two millennia ago. Because I now know beyond any inkling of doubt as to whom I serve, and in whom I dedicate my life with every breath I take." He wept unashamedly.

"Because, you see I have seen His face. And I have experienced a depth of forgiveness so great, that I will never, ever be the same again." He wagged his head as he spoke. "Never."

He paused, all the while exuding an air of ardent certainty. Then, in the stillness of the moment and fueled by the unquenchable fire of the Spirit, he drove the final nail.

"My dear friends, Jesus Christ is Lord of all creation, period! There is absolutely no other way by which man can come to God! So loving that he forfeited His own life willingly for us all and He asks only that in child-like faith, you place your trust in Him, just as I did! With my whole heart—my mind—my soul and strength.”

He pulled his glasses from his face and leaned heavily on the podium.

“My only regret is that it has taken me this long to tell you.”

Nineteen

Tuesday evening, April 7

The air was thick with consequences not fully defined. Not a sound came from the audience. Not a breath was taken, nor a whisper or sigh.

He looked out over the audience as two hundred plus pairs of eyes focused solely on him. It was as if they'd all had the wind knocked out of them at the same time, lacking the wherewithal to laugh or to scream. Finally one stolid clergyman jumped to his feet. "You've lost your mind," he squawked, wagging his skeletal fingers in complete and utter protest. Another man echoed his words and another joined in as the assembly erupted into chaos. Van Eaton held up his hand to stave off the inevitable hoopla, but there was nothing he could do now and he knew it. With a surgeon's precision, his words had dissected the bone from the marrow, the pagan from the saint, and the dedicated from the double minded. The room was now in so many pieces he wasn't even sure of how many divisions had been created. But not to worry; he knew God did, and that's all that truly mattered. And yet, his words unified many as well, though not as many as he supposed.

The people rose to their feet, many of them ranting wildly at the man who had breached the lines of tolerance more vehemently than anyone had ever dared. For there had always been that unwritten law—that professional courtesy that everyone associated with the religious caucus. The restraint was shared and rarely violated, if for no other reason than the obvious volatility of the subject. But Van Eaton had had enough of political correctness. He had come to know Christ as no other man for nearly twenty centuries, save his two friends, and there was no way he was going to remain silent about it.

"Please my friends, you must open your hearts to Him." He pressed his Testament to his chest. "There is not one here among us with whom He does not wish to have an intimate relationship! Not one! Please listen to me!"

† † †

After several contested minutes, the aged professor bowed his head and backed away from the podium. Visibly shaken, he quietly slipped behind the curtain and worked his way down the back stairway. Through the darkness he came to a door and pushed it open.

"So much for bipartisanism," came a voice from the shadows.

"Ms. Tabor?"

"Actually, I'm impressed," she said, stepping into the light. "Although it was rather Draconian even for you. I've never known you to be one to throw such caution into the wind." She pulled a recorder from her clutch and held it to his face. "Care to comment on what that was all about?"

Van Eaton scanned the hallway. "It was simply time," he said. "Long overdue in fact," his voice trailed off.

"Excuse me?"

"Off the record?"

She gave him the side-eye and depressed the power button. "If that's the way you want it."

"For now it is, yes," he continued while a glut of people poured into the hall. "Can we talk about this later?"

Tabor already had a business card in her hand with her room number scribbled on the back. "I'll be up." She slipped the card into his hand and gave him a wink.

Van Eaton's eyes narrowed. He couldn't even remember the last time he'd been hit on. But it also signaled a check in his spirit.

TWENTY

"You up?"

"Yeah." Paul rubbed his eyes and pulled the clock to his face. It was 10 p.m. "Elizabeth, is everything alright?"

"Yeah sure. I just wanted to let you know that I talked to Dr. Bernstein earlier this evening and asked him if I could get a work-up on a friend of mine."

There was a pause.

"Do what?"

"I said I asked Dr. Bernstein if I could get a consult on a friend of mine—as a personal favor to me."

The phone fell silent.

"On Peter!" Her voice noticeably rising.

"Yeah, I figured that's who you were talking about." Paul threw off the covers and sat on the edge of the bed. "What did he say?"

"He said he didn't think it would be a problem."

"Well that's good, isn't it?"

"It was, but then a few minutes later he called back and started asking more questions.”

“Like?”

“I don't know—like where was this person from? How long had I known him? That kind of stuff.”

“So what did you say?”

“I didn't know what to say, I just asked him if we could discuss it tomorrow.”

“And was he okay with that?”

“He seemed to be.”

“So what's the problem?”

“I don't know, I just want to do the right thing… and I don't want to start by lying.”

“Oh hon— you are so much like my wife it's scary.”

Twenty-One
Midnight, April 8

It was half past midnight when Professor Van Eaton lumbered up the palatial staircase, past ornamental iron railings and fluted marble pillars standing regally in the hotel's foyer. He pressed the elevator button and waited. A moment later the doors parted and he found himself face to face with Janis Tabor.

"Did you think you could get rid of me so easily?"

He stepped into the elevator without comment.

"So when am I going to get that story?"

He reached for the button and Tabor cut him off, pressing the button for her floor.

Janis Tabor had never married… nor even carried a torch as she often prided herself. Oh, there had been a few superficial brushes with romance, but on the whole, her career had taken precedence over everything. She decided early on that nothing would be as important. She did however nurture an extravagant side, which was more than obvious from her evening wear; a daring, red slash-front blouse that was a little more revealing than the occasion demanded, and a fitted black skirt that did so in all the right places.

"Do you think this is appropriate?" he asked.

Tabor slid the keycard through the slot and opened her door. "We're just going to talk, right?"

They entered her room and she wasted little time, sashaying over to the bar and pouring two glasses of Scotch. Van Eaton settled on the couch and Tabor sat next to him. She let her hair down and it cascaded smoothly over her shoulders. She was actually more of a looker than he'd first thought, but only a little more. She turned to him and met his eyes, hoping to draw him in.

Van Eaton tried to stay focused, not really knowing what she was up to.

"So what would you like to know?"

"Well, for starters, what's with all the *Jesus* talk? I thought you were an impartial soul." She spoke almost too casually, as if patronizing him.

Van Eaton drew a deep breath and let it out slowly. "You were there Miss Tabor. I thought my message was very clear."

"Maybe I'm a slow learner," she said with a wink.

"Well, I can explain it to you, but I can't understand it for you."

Tabor smirked. She crossed her legs and let her Prada pump dangle from her foot. Edging closer, she slid her toes up his trousers. Van pulled away politely.

"Miss Tabor, I uh—I'm flattered. I truly am—"

"Call me Janis."

He acquiesced rather than agreed. "Alright Janis, but this is hardly the time—"

She glanced away, feigning hurt feelings, but Van Eaton wasn't having any of it.

She's acting like she hasn't heard a word I've said all night, he thought. *Why now, at such a pivotal time as this? It's been literally less than an hour since I shared the most life-altering revelation, but for some reason, she persists. Does she really think she's going to convince me that she is genuinely interested in me? She is at least fifteen years my junior, maybe more.* But down deep inside he knew this was how the deceiver worked. He had just never been so cognizant of his tactics before.

"So tell me about your nomination, professor."

Van straightened and cleared his throat. "The Nobel?"

"Yes, of course." She produced a digital recorder and placed it on the coffee table in front of them. "All right, go ahead."

"The original application and submission was made by the university—"

"Georgetown?"

"Yes, but quite honestly, I didn't put a lot of credence into the whole affair. They make submissions every year."

"Come now professor, you don't really expect me to believe that do you? Besides, isn't there a million-dollar prize for the winner?"

Van Eaton stared at her strangely. "I suppose…" his voice trailed. "But the entire premise of my thesis, for all intents and purposes, is a moot point now."

"Oh, how so?"

"The *Errant Scriptures* was a study I pursued for all the wrong reasons, Miss—uh—Janis. Did you not hear a word I said at the conference tonight?"

She picked up his glass and handed it to him saying. "Here, catch up."

Van Eaton grimaced, bothered that she would even ask. "Nothing, thank you."

She lowered her chin and her deep-set eyes found his. "Do you find me attractive, professor?"

Van Eaton's face crimsoned instantly and he found it difficult to breathe. "Excuse me?"

"Do you find me attractive?" She repeated as if taunting him.

He glanced away impatiently. "Miss Tabor—"

"Janis," she corrected.

"Yes Janis, I suppose I do, but this is neither the time nor the place—"

She quietly sashayed to the door and slid the deadbolt into place, turned and let her blouse strap fall off her shoulder. "Oh, I think it's the perfect time."

† † †

Van Eaton stirred and awoke sluggishly. He sat up and for a moment he forgot where he was. As his head cleared, he was shocked to find himself in Janis Tabor's bedroom. He quietly found his shoes in the dark and shuffled across the room, following the light under the door that led to the living room.

Tabor sat on the couch; her legs tucked under her tightly as she typed furiously on her laptop. Van Eaton eased into the room and she abruptly closed her computer.

There was nothing more to say. No rhetorical questions. No sexual innuendos. She had acquired everything she'd gone after and Van Eaton was still reeling from the whole affair.

"I—I must be going." He glanced at his watch. It was 3 a.m.

Tabor pursed her lips to speak, but didn't.

He turned the handle and glanced back at her, wanting to say something, but he knew it was useless. He pulled the door shut behind him as Tabor opened her computer.

I-t'-s d-o-n-e.

Twenty-two
Wednesday morning, April 8

"I'm going to need a full work-up; Blood, urine, tox-screen," Elizabeth explained. The physician's assistant glanced at the paperwork and placed it on a stack of charts. Elizabeth plucked it from the pile and slid it back in front of her.

"Could we expedite this? Dr. Bernstein approved the work-up last night."

The PA took the papers and perused the form. "Peter Jonah. Hmmm. Mr. Jonah seems to have a rather obscure history." She looked at Elizabeth squarely, clicked her tongue and stamped the paperwork. "I'll order the blood work," she said. "Has he been assigned a room?"

"He's in the East sector. Room 210."

† † †

Van Eaton had just squeezed out the last of the toothpaste and spread it on his toothbrush when he noticed the message light on his phone. He lifted the receiver and dialed the message center.

You have one message marked urgent, the voice stated. *Please press zero to retrieve the message.*

He pressed the number and waited. The message was from Georgetown.

'Van Eaton…' the agitated voice belonged to Dean Armstrong. 'Well, you've finally gone and done it, haven't you?'

There was a pause, long enough that Van Eaton almost answered the recording.

'I've called a special meeting of the board to determine if you are still to be employed with the university,' he quipped. 'And don't think the prospect of the Nobel will save you either. I assure you it won't.'

The phone clicked and went silent. Van Eaton replaced the receiver and drew a deep breath. *News travels fast.*

TWENTY-THREE

Wednesday morning, April 8

"Liz, it's David. I need you to meet me over in the 'BC Unit'"

"Sure. Is something wrong?"

"Hardly—" he hinted. "Just come to the third floor again."

"Do I have time to stop by and check on Pete—Mr. Jonah?"

"This is *about* Mr. Jonah. He's here."

There was a pause.

"Is everything alright?"

"Just come as quickly as you can."

† † †

Elizabeth passed through the automated double doors and joined Bernstein at the sink.

"What's going on?"

"I'm not quite sure—" he said, "but I wanted you to be the first to see it."

Elizabeth looked at him quizzically.

He dried his hands and handed her a towel. "That's good

enough. This is precautionary, anyway. Follow me."

"No isolation gown?"

"Don't need it," he said.

Bernstein started down the hall while Elizabeth fell in behind, both at a good clip.

"What is going on?"

David stopped and propped against the handrail that ran the length of the hallway.

"First of all, good morning."

He glanced in both directions.

Seeing the coast was clear, he leaned over and gave Liz a quick kiss.

"I guess I shouldn't have done that… I hope you can forgive me."

"I forgive you for this transgression and any others you'd like to commit later. Now shall we put on our doctor hats?"

David smiled.

"So… what do you know about Mr. Jonah?"

Elizabeth gave a side-glance. "Well—as I told you before, he's a friend of the family. Why?"

"And you have family where?"

"Oh, ah, all over." Her words were obviously contrived.

"Elizabeth."

The young doctor hooked her glossy black hair around her ears and swapped stares with Bernstein. "Can we just leave it at that for now?"

"That's fine. Did you know he was dyslexic?"

"No, but that explains—" she stopped herself. "What else did you find?"

Bernstein clicked his pen and slid it into his pocket. "Your *friend* is in the next room," he admitted. "And he seems to have a rather unique ailment." He thought for a moment. "Perhaps ailment isn't the right word," he corrected. "Let's say, condition."

"I don't understand."

"You remember the old Bedouin you met yesterday?"

"Ali?"

"Yes, well Mr. Jonah seems to have many of the same markers as Ali and some of the same symptoms, but to a greater degree… a much greater degree, I might add."

Liz waited.

"Did you know that he has virtually no knowledge of modern medicine?" Bernstein tapped on his iPad. "In fact, he doesn't even know what we're talking about when we ask him anything about medical treatments, which seems rather odd considering he speaks such fluent English."

Elizabeth shrugged.

"But unlike Ali, his white blood cells are literally through the roof. In fact, I have never seen another human being with readings like these… and his platelets—" Bernstein handed her the iPad.

She scrolled through the lab results. "This can't be right."

"Oh, it's right. I've checked it a dozen times."

"And you did a CBC?"

"Yep."

"Chem panel?"

"Of course."

"What about Co-ags—the blood clots?"

"Ha! Oh yeah, the blood clots—look, before we go in you have to tell me who this guy is? What do you know about him?"

Elizabeth slid her hands in her pockets. "I told you. Peter is a friend of the family."

"A friend?"

"Yes, a friend."

"And when was the last time you had contact with your *friend* before you came to Israel?"

"I don't know. By letter I suppose." *Peter's books would have been letters, and I most certainly have read them over the last year,* she reasoned. She wondered why she was so consumed with telling the truth.

Bernstein felt as if he was being duped, but played along for the moment. "Well, either way, we have a situation here and I don't exactly know which way to go."

"What do you mean?"

He smiled and tapped on the door.

Peter lit up when he saw Elizabeth.

"Peter." She joined him at the bed. "Have they been treating you well?"

Peter smiled and placed his hand over hers. "Yes, I have been treated well," he answered guardedly. Small talk was still a bit strange to the big fisherman.

"I was telling Dr. Bernstein how we communicated by letter over the years." Elizabeth's eyes widened in hopes that Peter would catch on. Never mind the fact that he hadn't even written said letters yet, but she wasn't about to go there.

"Ah, the letters," Peter nodded.

Bernstein joined his patient on the other side and took him by the wrist. Peter recoiled slightly.

"He's just taking your pulse," Elizabeth said.

Peter stared incoherently.

"It's okay," she nodded.

Bernstein eyed his watch and waited—then typed in the numbers.

"How are you at drawing blood?"

"Okay I guess, why?"

He pulled a clear package from his pocket containing a syringe and handed it to Elizabeth. "Draw a vial from him."

She took the package and stared at it. "Why?"

"Trust me," he said with a 'you won't believe this' look on his face.

Elizabeth took an alcohol pad and swabbed the area, then tore open the package. "This may sting a little."

"I wouldn't count on it," Bernstein mumbled.

"What?"

"He seems to have an incredible tolerance to pain."

"Neuropathy?"

"No. He responds to the slightest touch, he just doesn't seem to associate pain."

Bernstein spoke as if Peter wasn't even in the room. It was just one of his quirks.

Elizabeth took Peter's wrist and patted the bend of his arm. "Nice veins. This should be easy enough." She gently slid the needle into the large vein and pulled the plunger, but there was no blood. "I'm usually better at this than that."

She tried again, apologizing to Peter who never even moved. Again, not a single drop of blood entered the needle. "Now I know I hit that vein." She inspected the needle as if it was defective. "That's got to be the largest Cephalic vein I've ever tried to hit."

"Oh I'm sure you hit it, but it doesn't make any difference," he explained. "You won't draw any blood out of it. Now, on top of that find your needle marks."

Elizabeth pulled Peter's arm to her face, glaring.

"You won't find them either," he said.

"Why?"

"Because they've already healed." Bernstein met her gaze and motioned toward the door. "A word?"

TWENTY-FOUR

Tuesday, April 7 – P.M.

The two doctors met in the hallway as Bernstein scrolled through several entries and typed something in. "Look at this."

Elizabeth focused on his notes.

"He has a red blood cell antigen that I didn't even know existed." Elizabeth envisioned her mouth dropping open even though it didn't.

"His cells regenerate like nothing I've ever seen in my life—like some sort of a super interloper with a protein enzyme that facilitates instantaneous healing."

Elizabeth took the iPad and studied the numbers. "Has he been typed yet?"

"That's just it, he doesn't have a type—at least not one that we know of."

"A, B, AB, O?"

"Not one of them. The only one remotely close is AB, but the enzyme levels in his blood don't even begin to compare."

Elizabeth tried to remain calm while she slipped in a silent prayer.

"Have you ever heard of *Neuregulin-1*?" Bernstein quizzed further.

"No."

"It's a regenerative molecule they've found in a salamander in southern Mexico and it appears that Peter may have the same strain. The thing regenerates its limbs after losing them literally within hours."

Elizabeth shook her head.

"And that's how your Peter is responding to our tests. Even when we tried to draw blood as you just did, we've found that it coagulates so quickly it can't be drawn with a syringe. We've even tried blood thinners, but they seem to have no effect on him."

"You're kidding me."

Bernstein wagged his head. "The only way we've been able to do any type of culture is to biopsy a particular area and run a culture on it… and even those areas have healed without so much as a scar."

"Really?"

"Yeah. In fact, this was so bizarre that I took the liberty of contacting an associate at Mount Olive," he admitted. "Elizabeth—they've offered to fly him to their facility in Baltimore."

"What? No. He's never—" Her words hung in the air for a moment.

"He's never what?"

They both held stares.

"He's never been out of the country."

"What's going on here Elizabeth?"

The young doctor's eyes glazed over at the thought as Bernstein went on.

"They say they can have their private jet here by the end of the week."

Elizabeth trembled slightly, kneading her brow.

"What about the CDC and all the Covid 19 issues we had to deal with not so long ago?"

"It's Mount Olive, Elizabeth. You know they're going to take every precaution. Besides, we both know he's not ill."

"Yeah."

"So what about his family?" he went on.

"He has no one."

"So it's settled then."

She walked to the window and watched an elderly man shuffle into the building. "He'll have to have a medical visa."

"That won't be a problem. You know that."

The two stood for a moment in reflective silence. "I'd like to discuss it with him tonight if I may," she said.

"Well of course. It's ultimately his decision anyway… but listen to me, if word of this leaks out, he'll have every drug company on the planet trying to make a play for him." His smile eroded as he considered the reality of his own words. "You do understand that if his blood enzyme can be replicated, it could be the medical discovery of the century… perhaps of all time. Just think of it Elizabeth—cancer, and not just one cancer, all cancers… eradicated. Heart disease, Aids even Covid19, all a thing of the past. There quite possibly would be no more disease of any kind on earth. None."

Elizabeth considered the gravity of Bernstein's words. With every syllable she could almost hear God whispering to her spirit.

TWENTY-FIVE
Wednesday morning, April 8

"Come in, professor." Tabor opened the door cautiously, knowing full well why he was there. Van Eaton made his way past her and toward the couch. She closed the door and propped her forehead against it. Finally she turned, a phony smile on her face.

"Miss Tabor—"

Tabor slinked toward the couch and sat down. She patted the cushion wanting him to sit, but he wasn't having any of it.

"Why are you doing this?"

"Whatever do you mean, professor?"

"Don't—" he bristled. "You know very well what I'm talking about." He unfolded the article he'd downloaded from the internet and handed it to her. "This is preposterous. And for the life of me, I don't even know why you would do such a thing."

Tabor took the paper and read the heading. *'Georgetown Professor Insults All Major Religions by Janis Tabor.'* She folded the article and handed it back to him.

"Are you really so naïve, professor?"

Van Eaton studied her face. "You seduced me for a story?"

Tabor feigned hurt feelings, but she wasn't very good at it. "The story was what I was after. Seducing you was just to prove I could."

"You are evil."

"Oh? Well you seemed to know what you were doing, as well. Don't act so innocent."

"You and I both know that nothing of any substance happened."

"That's your story."

"That's the truth."

"Well, whether anything happened or not isn't the point. The fact that you were here well into the night is enough to substantiate my story."

"So you're blackmailing me? For a story?"

"Call it what you want, but just remember I have the proof that you were here last night." She swiped the screen on her phone and revealed several incriminating photos.

Tears sprang to Van Eaton's eyes. "That speech was so very important to me." He buried his head in his hands.

Tabor strolled to the bar and twisted the cap off of a whiskey. "Come now professor, you know you're all alike," she grumbled. "And that's the problem, you're all such hypocrites."

"With all due respect Ms. Tabor, your problem is not with me," he said. "It's with God."

† † †

Tabor locked the door and spied her laptop. She had one new message marked urgent. It was from the United Bank of Nassau, Bahamas… a deposit in the amount of $75,000.

Twenty-six

Wednesday afternoon, April 8

Paul took a quick look through the peephole and unlocked the door.

"Well it's about time you two got here. I've been going stir crazy all day." He pulled Peter to his chest and hugged him smartly, then Elizabeth.

"Oh, I spoke with my wife today—" Paul said pulling the door shut. "She was happy that I'd made friends here in Israel. But this time thing is still messing with my head. We've been gone nearly a week and a half, but it's only been what—two days to her?"

Peter stared absently, retreating to thoughts of his own wife.

"You spoke with your wife?" Peter asked.

"Yes."

"And you spoke with her in another country?"

"Well… yes, I guess I did Peter," Paul said almost apologetically.

Elizabeth walked to the couch and sat down. "We've had quite a day," she confessed. Peter made his way to the sink and filled a glass with tap water just as if he'd been doing it all his life.

"So tell me about it."

Elizabeth slid to the edge of the cushion and draped her forearms across her knees. "It's been interesting to say the least, hasn't it, Peter?"

The apostle took a pull of his water and wiped his mouth on his sleeve. "From what I understand, yes."

"So tell me," Paul insisted.

"Well, I walked Peter through his evaluation this morning—" She went on sharing the incredible story of Peter's condition and the artistry of God's workings. And even though they all knew that God was in complete control, there was still the wonderment of witnessing His magnificent plan in progress.

"So Peter's blood is not like any other person's on earth?"

"It's truly an amazing thing isn't it?"

Paul wagged his head and looked at Peter with mixed emotions, a subtle anxiety creeping in. "And Johns Hopkins wants to study him?"

Elizabeth handed Paul the paperwork. "They've offered to admit him as soon as possible for the study and will handle everything… travel, housing, food, not to mention compensating him quite nicely for his time. But there is one caveat," she took the papers and flipped to the last page. "Right here it says they want exclusive rights—" She paused and met Peter's gaze. "To his blood."

"What?"

"That's exactly what *I* said. Actually it's the platelets in his blood they're after. The part of his blood that clots. It appears that Peter's blood has some sort of abnormal clotting factor with healing properties no one even knew existed."

"Abnormal?" Peter lowered his footrest and placed his feet on the floor.

"Oh, Peter I'm sorry," Elizabeth said. "I mean your blood is abnormal in that it has properties we've never seen before. Quite honestly, your blood appears to promote instantaneous healing."

Peter didn't really comprehend *instantaneous*, but he knew that something was happening that had never happened to him before.

"Have you ever had any issues with bleeding before… or trouble with bleeding?"

"No, I bleed as any other man. And I have the scars to prove it." He pushed up his sleeve and revealed two scars that ran the length of his forearm. "Fishing has its perils."

"But you would never have sustained scars with this condition," Elizabeth said as a chill snaked up her spine. "And yet you do have scars which tells me that this condition is new and that's what's facilitating all of this."

Paul smiled. "God is all over this."

"No doubt," Elizabeth admitted. "It's the perfect way to get him back to America, isn't it?"

"Absolutely," Paul said. "So there will be contracts and nondisclosures and so forth?"

"I'm sure. But I'll take care of all of that."

Paul turned to Peter. "So what do you think?"

Peter studied both of their faces until his mouth twisted into a grin. "It appears that my purpose for being here is being revealed."

The three sat without saying a word, considering all of the possibilities that lay ahead of them, not really knowing how to proceed, but sharing a peace that touched all of their hearts equally.

Finally Paul stood and cinched up his pants. "So they've offered to fly our brother to Mount Olive Hospital in Baltimore, huh?"

Elizabeth nodded. "Yep—provided I get the completed paperwork back to them, which shouldn't be a problem. I've already put in a call to my boss, Ray Roaten. Oh, and we'll be allowed to accompany him as well." Elizabeth grinned, knowing more than she let on.

"You're kidding." Paul sank back into his chair. "Have you heard from the professor? I wonder how he's doing?"

Twenty-Seven

Wednesday, April 8

Professor Van Eaton paced the floor nervously, waiting for the call he feared most likely would be the end his career. Assuming the worst, he gathered the clothes in his drawer and stuffed them into his suitcase along with the bloodstained mantle he had no intention of ever parting with. He took it and sank down on the disheveled bed.

Why had this woman done such a thing? He thought. *What purpose could there possibly be in threatening to discredit me in such a way? I am a different man now!* He sighed and pulled a pillow over his face. "Why is this happening to me?" he cried.

After several grueling minutes he sat up and spied the mini bar at the end of the credenza. He grabbed the handle and pulled, but it was as if something kept the door from opening, or maybe it was just his own conscience. Either way, he knew a fight was brewing, and he was feeling strangely outnumbered.

TWENTY-EIGHT
Wednesday, April 8

"Can I get you a coffee?"

"No thank you."

"Water?"

"Yes please."

He handed her a bottle of Evian and purposely touched her hand. Her heart fluttered.

"Please take a seat." Bernstein motioned to the chair. He flipped open the hospital ops manual and began to read. "'Persons who wish to attain a Medical Visa in order to enter into the United States for medical treatment must satisfy specific social and economic ties with not only their home country, but the destination country, as well.'" He closed the book and cupped his hands over it. "Now as I see it, we should be able to handle Mr. Jonah's affiliation with Israel, but—"

Elizabeth nodded cautiously. "But you need an anchor baby."

Bernstein couldn't help but laugh. "Not exactly. Well, maybe." He stood and clasped his hands behind his back and gazed out his office window. "Mount Olive has already submitted the necessary paperwork to the American Consulate here in Jerusalem, but the entire process requires documentation from a physician, in this case an American, to sign an I-133 affidavit. That's a verification of support in the United States before the transfer can be made."

Elizabeth smiled. "So where do I sign?"

"Not so fast Liz." His casual familiarity caught her off guard. She glanced away as he continued.

"I want you to think about what you're doing because there is more to it than what you might think. They require a copy of your income tax records, in some cases bank statements, Homeland Security has to run a background check and so on." Bernstein moved closer to Elizabeth and spoke just above a whisper. "But if this thing with Mr. Jonah turns out the way I think it might, there is no telling where it may lead."

Elizabeth smiled. *If you only knew.*

"So is that it?"

Bernstein slid into the chair behind his desk. "Well, not exactly."

For a moment he waited, then with deference he continued. "I know there is something more here than meets the eye and I need you to tell me what it is."

In the blink of an eye, it felt as if all the air had been sucked out of the room. Elizabeth tried not to tip her hand, but it was more than obvious that she was holding something back.

"Dr. Bernstein."

"David," he insisted.

Elizabeth's eyes flitted to his and the two shared a moment. There was chemistry there for sure, but it was more than that and they were both aware of it.

"David. I—I don't know what to say."

Bernstein could tell from her tone that she was hiding something, but he couldn't connect the dots. In his spirit though, he sensed it.

TWENTY-NINE

Wednesday, April 8

Elizabeth stirred a packet of creamer into her coffee and glanced at Peter, remembering the first time she'd offered him the brew. And the fact that it happened literally days ago, and yet intertwined with events that had occurred centuries before, only added to the mystery.

From across the room she watched the apostle as he sat in front of the TV. Like any ordinary male on the planet, he stared at it in wonder. In fact, if she hadn't known better, she would have assumed that was exactly who he was—just an ordinary *Joe* glued to the set. He even clutched the remote like a pro. But she knew this man was anything but ordinary, and his interests far outreached the events on the screen, which at the moment was an automobile commercial.

"Shouldn't the professor be back here in the next day or two?" Elizabeth cradled her cup and sipped.

"As far as I know."

"Well, that works out perfect, too. They said that there is room on the plane for the patient and up to five more."

Peter sat up in his chair. "The patient?"

Elizabeth grinned. "That would be you."

Peter scratched his head and his bushy eyebrows rose.

"What do you think will happen when we get there?" Paul added.

Elizabeth shrugged. "I don't know exactly, but I know the Lord does."

Paul just gazed at her with wonder. "God has really done a work in you, hasn't He?"

Elizabeth sipped her brew and the two exchanged smiles.

† † †

The shrill tone of the telephone grew louder, echoing off the inside of Van Eaton's skull. He lifted the receiver and pulled it to his ear. "Hellllo." His voice slurred into the handset.

"Professor?"

Van Eaton coughed and sat up. "Paul?" He tried not to breath, as if Paul could have smelled the liquor on his breath.

"Yes, is everything all right?"

Van Eaton rubbed his eyes and focused on the clock beside the bed. It was 7:30 p.m. He'd been asleep all day.

"Uh, yes, everything's fine. Are you all right? Is everything all right there?"

"We're all good Van. We just need to talk. Something's come up."

Van Eaton felt the fatigue slip away. "What's wrong?"

"Nothing is wrong, it's just that—" Paul's emotions were telling, even over the receiver. "It appears that God has opened the door to get Peter to America. And all of us with him."

Van Eaton glanced in a mirror at his reflection. He looked like a haggard drunk and it embarrassed him. "I'm glad for you Paul—for all of you."

Paul pulled the receiver from his ear and looked at it strangely.

"You're glad for us? Professor, you're part of us."

Van Eaton combed his fingers through his hair and Paul could hear him sobbing.

"What's wrong brother?"

Van Eaton drew a deep breath and exhaled.

"Professor—"

"It's none of your business," he shot back.

Paul winced at his words, but quickly recovered.

"I've got another call coming in," Van Eaton admitted. "I must call you back."

"Please do," Paul said. "And professor—"

"Yes?"

"I love you brother. Whatever's going on, we'll get through it."

Van Eaton choked up and could barely answer. "I have to go."

Paul walked into the room and quietly sat down.

"What's wrong, Paul?"

"Something's wrong with the professor."

"What do you mean?"

"I don't know, he cut me off before we had a chance to talk about it… said he had to take another call."

"What do you think it is?"

Paul's eyes inched up to Elizabeth's. "I don't know, but he sounded like the old Van Eaton."

"That's not good," she said somberly.

"No, it's not."

Van Eaton pressed the button and the call switched over.

"Yes?"

"Van Eaton?"

"Yes, Dean."

"Well, I don't know how you did it, but somehow you were granted a stay of execution." *Dean Armstrong was never one to pull any punches, no matter how much they hurt,* Van Eaton thought. *And if he didn't like you—God help you.*

"Excuse me?"

"Don't be coy with me professor. Just know that there is a called meeting of the faculty delegates next Monday to discuss the remainder of your tenure here at Georgetown. And you *will* be in attendance."

"But I was not scheduled to be back at the university until the 15th."

"As of today, the remainder of your trip has been effectively cancelled," he said as if passing sentence. "I suggest you make arrangements to get back here as soon as possible."

"But—" The phone went silent.

THIRTY

Wednesday evening, April 8

Peter's eyes drifted to the TV playing in the background and he struggled to focus. In his own way he knew that God was responsible for his trek into the future and the remarkable events that had occurred over the past few days—but it was impossible not to marvel at the plethora of modernisms that flooded his psyche; television, cellular phones, busses, even air-conditioning was such a strange phenomenon that he hardly knew how to respond. Running water, electricity, the list was endless. Again he focused on the TV:

> *Sources tell us that attorneys representing the Muslim students at Georgetown University and numerous Catholic universities across the nation are protesting that Christian symbols displayed in the schools are offensive and claim they violate their religious rights as Muslims. Monsignor Joseph Sergetti, spokesman for the National Catholic Diocese Association was quick to point out that Georgetown is a private Catholic university and therefore reserves the right to follow its*

own religious rites. Monsignor Sergetti, of the famed St. Patrick's Cathedral in New York City...

"*Cath-o-lik.* I have heard this word a number of times. What exactly does it mean?" Peter asked innocently.

Elizabeth stood and stretched. "I'll let you take this one," she said to Paul. "I need to make a phone call, anyway."

Paul cleared his throat and thought for a moment. "Well, the word Catholic actually means church. It's Latin, I believe. And a religion... probably the largest religion in the world."

"This is religion?" Peter pressed the off button on the remote and clasped his hands over his chest. "And you are Catholic?"

"No, actually, I'm Baptist."

"And this is another religion?"

"Yes. We are called Protestants."

"Pro-tes-tants?"

"Yes."

"The name suggests discord."

Paul guffawed. "Yeah, I guess it does."

"And what of the Jews? What is their place in this 21st century?"

Paul considered the question for a moment.

"Here we go—"

† † †

"Lufthansa Airlines, Gurnard speaking." The accent combined with the sound system made the announcement almost too garbled for Van Eaton to understand.

"I need to see about changing my flight. Confirmation GBQ287, Leonardo Van Eaton."

"Yes, I'll check that for you sir. Yes... the next flight departs in the morning at 9:25, Washington Dulles, via Tel Aviv to Atlanta."

"Nothing direct?"

"Checking. No sir, I am sorry."

"Fine. Just book it," Van Eaton huffed. He wrote down the confirmation number and replaced the handset.

I guess I'm going to Israel whether I like it or not.

THIRTY-ONE

Wednesday evening, April 8

"I just got off the phone with Ray Roaten. He sounded like he was miffed that I was considering coming home early," Elizabeth said. She glanced over at Peter who was engrossed in a TV program. She lowered her voice. "By the way, I have a surprise."

Paul wrapped his arms around himself in a defensive stance. "Another surprise?" he asked with trepidation.

Liz punched him in the arm. "Stop it! I'm being serious."

"Okay, what?"

"Bernstein says he's dyslexic." She motioned toward Peter.

Paul stifled his laughter! "Thank goodness! I couldn't take any more shocks!" he whispered heavily. "Dyslexic?"

"Yeah."

"How did they find that out?"

"I don't know, we didn't really get into it. It doesn't matter anyway. I just thought it was interesting."

"Yeah. So what did you tell Roaten?"

"I just said we had a case that Dr. Bernstein wanted me to be involved with. He's probably just jealous that I'll be working with

Mount Olive."

"Well, I hope it won't have any repercussions for you," Paul said.

"I don't think it will, but if it does that's okay too. God's got this."

Paul grinned. "No doubt."

† † †

Paul poured a cup of coffee and handed it to Peter. "So as I was saying, America—the United States, is a world power… as of today, *the* world power, albeit there are those who wouldn't have it that way."

"Your *Amerika* sounds much like Rome," Peter confessed.

"In some ways, it is like Rome," Paul surmised. "But the Rome you knew has long since passed… many centuries ago."

Peter shook his head. Surprises were becoming less and less of a shock to him. "Was Rome defeated?"

"They sort of imploded sometime after the third or fourth century—after Constantine, who was actually the first Christian Caesar."

Peter sank back in his seat. "A Christian Caesar."

"It's really getting late you guys," Elizabeth covered her mouth and yawned. "And we've only got one day left before we have to leave. I wouldn't mind visiting a few of the sights—if you guys were up for it."

"I'd love to, but you know tomorrow is—" Paul glanced at Peter, "Passover. And we leave on *Good Friday*." He grimaced as he spoke the words.

"*Good Friday?*" Peter repeated.

Paul wavered for a moment. "It's the Christian celebration— of the crucifixion." An awkward silence descended on the three.

"The world celebrates the crucifixion?"

Paul glanced at Elizabeth, as if seeking approval. "The

crucifixion—was the pivotal event of the Christian faith," he explained with gentle prowess.

Peter frowned. "But—but how can our loving Savior being tortured by the people He loves be called good?"

Paul continued guardedly. "It is good because Jesus accomplished his mission. The last words He uttered from the cross were, 'It is finished.' And in that moment, all sin, past, present and future was atoned for."

Paul plucked his Bible from the counter and thumbed through it. "Isaiah foretold it here in chapter 53. "'By His stripes we are healed,'" he read. "His wounds were literally our healing. His blood paid our ransom and created a path of redemption for all who believe."

Peter simply stared at Paul. "This is so much to consider," he spoke with a somber tone. "I am beginning to understand the depth of the sacrifice the Master paid. God's plan of redemption was carried out on the cross—" he spoke as if there was sudden illumination. "We thought… John and Andrew, all of us that Jesus was going to establish His kingdom here on earth."

Paul smiled reassuringly. "We have to remember that you came with us to the future before many pivotal events had occurred," he said. "None of us knows exactly how all of this will work out, but for sure God does."

Peter nodded slowly. "And all of the events that led to the crucifixion? They are documented Biblical entries?"

"Yes, of course," Paul assured.

Peter quietly stood with effort. "I would like to lie down for a while." He walked to the door of his bedroom and stopped. "Am I remembered as being a coward?"

Paul and Elizabeth immediately came to him. "Don't do this to yourself Peter. You are a great man and the world remembers you as a great man."

The apostle managed a strained smile and placed his hand on Paul's shoulder. "His love truly covers a multitude of sins…"

† † †

"Is he asleep?"

"Yeah, I covered him up."

"I hate to hear him talk like that," Elizabeth sighed. "I feel so sorry for him."

Paul poured the last of the coffee into his mug. "You know, I'm beginning to think that there's more going on here than we may understand."

Elizabeth nodded.

"This condition of his—do you think he had it before he came back with us? To the future I mean?"

"I don't know."

"You think this is part of the plan?"

Elizabeth's eyes glistened as she looked at Paul. "I can't help but think that it is," she said in a soft, but confident voice.

Paul gazed back at her, then past, feeling a surge of calm with her words. "There you go again. You're sitting there with all the faith of a child and I am over here trying to figure out all the details, like how we're going to meet back up with Van Eaton. He's not supposed to be back here until Saturday."

"Well, maybe he's not supposed to go back with us at all. Maybe he's done everything he was supposed to do." There was a short silence. "But that's not what I want."

Paul's worry was replaced with a cautious smile. "Me neither."

Thirty-two

Wednesday evening, April 8

"Caesarea Philippi is just ahead Master," Peter announced. "Should we prepare for the night here?"

Jesus looked around. "This is a good place."

The two sons of Zebedee began offloading the donkey while the other disciples either gathered wood for a fire, went for water or any number of other duties; each man took on his own responsibility. This was how they had operated for nearly three years and Peter assumed that it would likely continue, unless of course, the Master had other ideas. The real question on most of their minds though was why Jesus hadn't already begun the task of enlisting mercenaries for the establishment of His kingdom? It only made sense. Even Simon, the only named Zealot in the group had alluded to it on more than one occasion, but Jesus never seemed to be interested in listening to him when he talked that way.

A roaring fire crackled and swirled into the pale night sky as the group of weary disciples huddled close. The nights had been unseasonably cold even though winter had passed, but they all knew it wouldn't be long before the nights would be considerably warmer and the fires smaller, but for now bigger was certainly better.

After the meal Jesus called His chosen few to gather around Him. He had something special He wanted to share with them—something He'd harbored in His heart for a very long time.

His back to the fire, His silhouette created a ghostly halo against the flame and smoke, and in a strange way set the mood. For a moment He stood in silence, gazing into each man's face and thus into their hearts as he considered the journey that lay ahead of them. He knew Jerusalem would be His final destination on earth and a trap of sorts was being laid, but it was a trap He would willingly endure, even knowing that He wouldn't come through it alive. And even though He possessed the power to overcome any obstacle that man could lay for Him, the incarnate Christ chose to set aside His own divine strengths.

In truth, it had been more than thirty years since He'd relinquished those virtues theologians would eventually label omnipotence, omniscience and even omnipresence. He willingly surrendered them all to become human. And with that decision came the limitations of humanity and even mortality itself. In some ways it seemed a curse. The divergence of deity with humanity had created a strange sort of irony never before confronted by any living being. The limitless became limited and the infinite, finite. God had literally wrapped Himself in human flesh to become a man, but now His earthly life was drawing to a close and He was fully aware of it. Yet by the same token He was at perfect peace. Being at the right hand of the Father had begun to permeate His thoughts on a regular basis to the point that He had literally become homesick. It was something He had shared with no one, but it was more than apparent if for no other reason than the appearance of His countenance. Even His body language was telling had His disciples known to look for it, but sadly their eyes remained focused on their own agendas.

"Who do people say the Son of Man is?" Jesus asked, a sense of urgency spilling into His voice.

"What are you saying, Master?" Peter finally asked.

Jesus stroked His beard and His eyes wandered. "The people. Who do they say I am?"

Exchanges of glances swept through the group, but no one was quick to answer. In fact, they had all learned early on that quick answers were usually wrong answers.

"Some say John the Baptist," John finally admitted, knowing full well that Jesus was not John because he had followed the Baptist himself before coming to Jesus.

"Others say Elijah," another said. This brought on a few snickers seeing as Elijah had lived hundreds of years earlier.

"Some others even say Jeremiah or one of the prophets." This brought on even more laughter.

Jesus remained focused. "But what about you?" He asked pointedly. "Who do you say that I am?"

The question hung in the air for a moment, like a butterfly that no one was willing to touch. And for several long moments no one did.

Then Peter came forward, compelled solely by the innermost yearnings of the Spirit. "You are the Christ," he said emphatically. "The Son of the living God." Peter's words came with a confidence that even he hadn't known before. Caught up in the moment, he lowered himself to his knees and bowed his face to the ground.

A compassionate smile inched across Jesus' face, simply because He knew Peter followed his heart, and he did so without fear of reproach.

"Blessed are you, Simon son of Jonah, for this was not revealed to you by man, but by my Father in heaven."

Jesus then took him by the hand and pulled him to his feet while the others looked on. "And I tell you that you are Peter, and upon this rock I will build my church, and the gates of Hades will not overcome it. And I will give you the keys of the kingdom of

Heaven…"

Peter bolted straight up in the bed. Squinting through the still darkness with tear-filled eyes, he cried with joy. He gently turned back the covers and slid to his knees beside the bed.

"He will give me the keys of the kingdom of Heaven…" he whispered heavily. "But what does this mean?"

Thirty-Three

The early morning hours were a silent witness to Elizabeth who sat on a narrow, cast-iron balcony attached to her hotel room. Nursing a hot cup of *Earl Grey* she hugged her knees to her chest and gazed out over the city. It had been a whirlwind four days since returning from their adventure to the past, and the realization that they were spending their last day in Israel had made sleep the furthest thing from her mind. She sipped her brew and considered the day. Having arranged with Bernstein that she would spend her last day in Israel in the old city, she didn't want to waste a single minute. The city was two thousand years older now and she wanted to view things from her new perspective. In particular, she and Paul both wanted to visit the Garden Tomb. They had been whisked forward in time before that part of the story had come to fruition and the absence of that single event had created a strange sort of conundrum that still weighed heavily on their hearts.

† † †

The Indira Gandhi International Airport had two very distinct aromas: body odor and curry. At least that's how Van Eaton perceived it. Dressed in a tweed jacket with elbow patches and pleated khaki trousers, the elder scholar hoisted his bags onto a cart and slid two rupees into the slot. He wrestled a luggage cart off the track and wheeled it toward the gate.

He was dreading the day. And no matter how hard he tried, there was no getting around the fact that, at some point, he was going to have to face his friends—and of course, Peter. How could a man whose life had literally been touched by the living Christ have been so easily turned upside down? He was a spirit-filled man—or so he thought—who followed Christ with breathless resolve. Yet he now found himself in a situation where he may not only lose his job, but possibly his career. Then adding insult to injury, he'd tried to bury his shame in a bottle. It made no sense. How could he have fallen so easily? But worst of all, he was terrified that he was slipping back into the *old man* he thought was long gone. The disgruntled, pessimistic academic everyone had come to accept, or at the very least tolerate, was slowly returning and it seemed there was nothing he could do to stop it.

† † †

Paul donned his canvas *Hey Dudes* and slipped a bottled water into his fanny pack. He spied his video camera beside the TV and huffed. *Not this time*, he thought.

Across the room, Peter slid on his shirt and fumbled with the buttons—meticulously fastening each one until he reached the bottom. With one button off, he tucked it in anyway.

"We'll Uber over to Elizabeth's hotel and go on to the Garden Tomb from there." Paul talked to Peter as if he knew what an Uber was. Peter simply nodded.

The dawn burned away the darkness as Paul, Elizabeth and

Peter traveled around the northwest quadrant of the old city, taking in the sights, fleeting as they were. Past the massive stone ramparts of the Jaffa Gate they followed the pot-holed street that led past the Citadel, its blocks of smooth limestone looming majestically against the morning sun. And even though it was early morning, people marched in all directions, as if nothing so important had ever occurred in this wonderful place. How very odd it seemed to Elizabeth, as well as Paul who sat and watched the sights spill by. And of course Peter, who was sandwiched between the two, took it all in without saying a word.

"The Garden Tomb *vill* be just ahead," the driver said in a heavy Middle Eastern accent. His only notable feature was a scraggly goatee that hung from his pointed chin… with bits of breakfast in it.

Minutes later they pulled up to, of all places, a bus station—and an Arab one at that. They soon learned from the driver that the entire northern section of the old city was known as the Arab Quarter. Paul thanked him and selected 5 stars on his Uber text while Peter and Elizabeth stepped onto the curb.

The pathway leading to the Garden Tomb was a narrow landing of worn wooden planks fixed to rusted metal framing. It snaked around the back of the terminal, and up a hill that emptied into a wooded courtyard. To their immediate right, a jagged hillside loomed, its unmistakable face resembling that of a misshapen skull. They all looked on as if it begged them to remember.

"The hill is the same," Peter spoke softly. He pressed his face to the chain link fence that separated them from *The Skull* as he had come to know it. Oddly enough, it appeared almost identical to when they followed Jesus to the top in those final hours, Elizabeth realized. For a moment she worried for Peter who stood in silence, his eyes wandering up and down the rocky crag as he relived the day.

"Ironic, is it not?"

The three turned in unison at the voice whose 'R's rolled so eloquently.

"Excuse me?"

"Golgotha. Do you not find it ironic that this most sacred ground lies within Muslim control?"

"I had no idea," Elizabeth confessed.

The sixtyish man with the round face and the large round nostrils smiled broadly. "Yes. There are Muslim graves dating back many centuries that lie atop Golgotha—" he pointed to the crest of the hill, "which renders the land Muslim essentially by association."

The man extended his hand. "My name is Yousef," he said. "I am the curator here at the Garden Tomb."

"I'm Elizabeth and this is Peter and Paul."

They all exchanged handshakes.

"Ah, such noteworthy, biblical names. Can you imagine meeting Peter and Paul here in the Holy Land?"

Paul traded not only winks, but giggles with Elizabeth and Peter. *You don't know how close you are brother,* they both mused.

"And you are a physician, no?" He looked directly at Elizabeth.

"Yes, but how—"

"I was visiting a friend at Rashaman Hospital yesterday."

"Of course."

"And you?" he motioned to Peter. "You are a physician also?"

"No," Peter said curtly. His people skills were not quite what they should be but he was getting there.

"So, would you all care to visit another of the most sacred parcels in Israel?"

Smiles immediately wreathed their faces.

† † †

The day seemed uncharacteristically quiet as they followed the stately curator up the landing that ultimately emptied into a wooded courtyard, replete with age-old olive trees and sculpted shrubbery littering the grounds throughout. Even the ground itself, though laden with pea-gravel was artfully landscaped and well maintained.

"Just ahead, you will find the Garden Tomb," Yousef motioned on ahead. He glanced at his watch and seemed pleased. "And now I will leave you to your journey. Spend as long as you like at the sepulcher. It will be an experience like no other." Then he bowed modestly and shook their hands. As he turned and disappeared through the trees, not one of them noticed he cast no shadow.

Thirty-Four

Thursday morning, April 9

On the far side of the grounds, the stone laden entrance to the sepulcher came into view. Descending the stairway, Paul wished he'd brought his video camera, but was content to snap pictures and a short video with his phone just the same.

The scene was picturesque. The exterior of the sepulcher itself consisted of a three by five opening hewn from the face of a rocky crag. The entire right side of the opening, having partially collapsed at the turn of the century, was supported with limestone blocks that had been placed to prevent further damage. In fact, Elizabeth had read those stones had been set there as far back as the 1890's and were still holding strong.

In front of the entrance and at its base, a channel that ran the length of the tomb was carved out of the limestone in order to funnel a large, circular stone in front of the entrance. Paul knew from his studies that this was how many sepulchers were fashioned in Jesus' day, utilizing a stone to be rolled in front of the doorway to keep out thieves as well as scavenging animals. And of course the scriptures were clear that a stone was placed in front of the original tomb, but there was no stone in place here, only remnants of what had been. *Maybe people from past pilgrimages had chipped away pieces of the stone over the years,* he surmised. He'd read of other such pilfering of artifacts in the Holy Lands over the centuries and that it was quite common.

Standing at the entrance, the three had their own visions of what had occurred there so long ago… or only days ago. Nonetheless, they all imagined the lifeless body of the Savior as He was laid to rest in the tomb and the utter despondency of those who followed Him—Peter being one of them.

Paul turned to the lone disciple, a plethora of thoughts assaulting his brain as to what Peter must truly be experiencing. But, rather than mentioning it, he whispered a silent prayer. Finally the three stepped inside.

In the cool, dank air of the empty tomb they stood without a word spoken between them—only the soft ins and outs of breathing and slight moans that the imagination of so great an event brought with it. On the wall, Peter noticed a hand-carved wooden plaque that hung just inside the entrance—and the only modern artifact there. It read: HE IS NOT HERE, FOR HE IS RISEN!

Peter traced the letters with his fingers.

"'He is not here, for He is risen,'" Paul read aloud.

Peter stroked the smooth walls and imagined Jesus being there. For a moment he could almost feel *His* presence. His touch. The warmth of His smile. It was as if He was there as surely as they.

In the stillness, Peter sank to his knees and discreetly removed his sandals. He bowed his face to the stone floor and kissed it, again and again, all the while bathing it with his tears.

Paul and Elizabeth joined him at the floor—and the three coupled hands. In the tender moment, Paul tried to voice a prayer, but no words could suffice.

Finally Peter sat up and rubbed his eyes as his face flushed. "Memories are forming of events I have yet to experience." He stared in the air between Paul and Elizabeth. "I remember running to the tomb—and John with me, but Jesus was not here." Peter's words seemed foreign even to him. "But how can this be? I am recalling events that had not occurred."

"But they did Peter," Elizabeth admitted. "The Bible says that's exactly what happened."

"And the tomb was destroyed?"

"What?"

"The tomb… it was destroyed."

Paul looked strangely at Elizabeth. "No… not to my knowledge."

Peter was suddenly filled with a sense of urgency. "We must go—now!"

The three stepped outside into the stark sunlight as Peter heaved a long, deep breath.

"Hold on, I left my bag—" Elizabeth turned and ran back inside.

† † †

The cell phone vibrated once before he answered.

"They are all together?"

"Yes."

"And the apostle?"

"He is with them."

"Good. You know what to do."

Yousef punched in a series of numbers and discretely slipped the burner phone into a trashcan as he hurried off the grounds.

THIRTY-FIVE
Thursday morning, April 9

A symphony of sirens resonated for miles as emergency vehicles picked their way through the crowded streets and converged at the boardwalk leading to the Garden Tomb.

The blast encompassed the entire upper structure of the sepulcher, spraying rocks and debris the length of a football field through the streets of the Arab Quarter, slamming men, women and children to the ground from the sheer concussion alone. Through the dense smoke and rubble, Peter somehow managed to find Paul.

"Are you injured?"

"I'm just shaken up. Wh—where's Elizabeth?"

Peter turned and disappeared into the haze. A minute later he emerged with Elizabeth cradled in his arms. He lowered her to the ground as Paul slid his hand to the small of her neck and brushed her hair out of her face. She was barely conscious.

"My hand—" she whispered.

Paul pushed up her blood-soaked sleeve. "We've got to get help—"

"No." Peter quickly surveyed their surroundings, as if confirming they were alone. He focused on Elizabeth, then her hand. "Do you trust me?"

Elizabeth's eyes rose to meet his. "You know I do," her words were breathy and weak.

Peter took her mangled hand and covered it with his own.

"For your glory Father… and for the sake of Christ."

The words were barely spoken when Elizabeth shuddered and cried out as the pain intensified. Her skin flushed hot and she watched as her hand moved involuntarily. Blinking away the tears, she forced herself to watch as muscles formed over bone and tendons over muscle. She wanted to throw up, but was too absorbed in the sight to give in.

Paul looked on in silence. He'd never witnessed anything like this in all of his life.

† † †

As the two men helped Elizabeth to her feet, two *MADA* agents appeared through the haze.

"Is anyone hurt?"

Elizabeth looked at Peter knowing they shared a secret. "I think we're okay." She went on to brush off her clothes with *both* hands. "What's happened?"

"If I was to speculate, I would say Hamas. We have been on alert since the killing in the Gaza Strip yesterday. Are you sure none of you are injured?" He noticed Peter's clothing was peppered with holes, but he appeared to be unharmed.

"Yes we are all fine," they all confirmed.

"And are there others?"

"There was no one else around that we know of—" Paul said as another man approached.

"Is everyone all right?"

"We are all fine. What happened to the—to Yousef?"

"Who?"

"The curator. We met him at the entrance when we got here."

The man looked strangely at the three. "My apologies sir, but I am the curator."

Thirty-six

Thursday afternoon, April 9

'*... the blast occurred at approximately 9:40 a.m. this morning here in the area known as the Arab quarter of the old city. Sources tell Knesset TV that the blast encompassed an entire city block, raining debris hundreds of yards in all directions and even on tourists and street vendors as far south as the Damascus Gate. There were also initial reports that there had been a group of Americans injured in the blast, but those reports are still unsubstantiated at this time. There have also been various reports that Hamas may be claiming responsibility, but as of yet we have no confirmed reports...*'

Paul shoveled double the amount of coffee into the filter and pressed the start button on the coffee maker. He turned to Elizabeth who sat at the bar with Peter. "I honestly don't know what to think," he confessed. "Was that bomb meant for us or was it just a coincidence we were there?"

"Have you ever heard that coincidence is just God remaining anonymous?"

"No—but I like it. That's the first thing that's made sense today."

Peter looked strangely at them both.

"*Coincidence* means by chance," Elizabeth explained.

Peter nodded. "Oh."

"But how did you know to keep her from going back in the tomb?" Paul asked.

"I have no clear answer for this. I only knew that something was wrong. And then there was the memory I spoke of. That I was running to the tomb. It was then I came to understand that I was not running *to* the tomb—but *from* it. And I knew we were in danger."

Elizabeth wagged her head. "Unbelievable."

"I've also been wondering about that guy—Yousef? You think he had anything to do with it?" Paul asked.

"I don't know," Elizabeth said, unconsciously stroking her hand, "but I thank God you were there with us Peter. From keeping me going back in there—and what you did to my—my hand!" She rotated her hand from front to back to front again. "Without so much as a scar!"

Peter sighed. A subtle anxiety reached to his very core. "I—I do not know what to say. The Master was always the healer. He had said we would acquire the power someday, but I do not know if any of us truly believed it." He stared vacantly for a moment. "I watched Him heal the sick, the lame, the demented—even my own wife's mother, but I had no power to perform such miracles," he admitted.

"Well that's obviously not the case now," she said. "Not to mention your shirt Peter. It's riddled with holes but you're completely unscathed! It truly is a miracle."

As they spoke, Paul's mind drifted to the scriptures… to his studies in Acts. *How many sermon series have I preached on this very subject?* he thought. *Peter healed numerous times… but why does he not believe—oh my gosh. No he hasn't.*

Paul caught Elizabeth's eye and gave a side-eye toward the couch.

"Would you excuse us?"

Peter nodded. "I have to, uh—" He walked toward the bathroom as Paul and Elizabeth swapped smiles. They waited until he closed the door.

"I'm afraid he's right," Paul said just above a whisper. "I didn't understand why he had no knowledge of healing the sick when the book of Acts tells of his healings… Tabitha, the lame man, people were even bringing the sick into the streets so that his shadow might fall on them and heal them, but none of that had happened yet. We came back before he had a chance to do any of those things."

Elizabeth hung on Paul's every word. And even though she had known him literally less than two weeks, she had a true admiration for him, believing him to be a scholar in his own right. "But he said he was remembering things he had no previous knowledge of!"

"I know right? When he told us that, I thought my head was going to explode!" Paul tried to keep his voice down. "But here's the scary part, I don't know how much I'm supposed to share with him now. I mean—it's more than obvious that God is in control here—I'll never doubt that again as long as I live, but I want to share some things with him—those things that came to define him as the man of God he truly was—or is. Mercy!"

Elizabeth studied her manicure, which was hideous. "We have been going back and forth about this for the last two weeks Paul. This is your area of expertise." She reached and took hold of his forearm. "But I still believe that God will show us what to do. I'm just glad the professor wasn't with us. I don't know if he would have fared as well as we did."

"No, I don't think he would have either. The old codger."

Elizabeth grinned.

"That is quite a Mikvah." Peter stepped out of the bathroom and wiped his hands on his pants.

"You know, I think it's just about time we talked about

another modern convenience, Peter." Elizabeth reached through the bathroom door for the sink. "We call this soap."

Thirty-Seven

Thursday morning, April 9

"Something to drink sir?"

The aged scholar turned to the flight attendant without making eye contact. "Nothing, thank you." He turned back to the window and slipped back into his thoughts. He would be landing in Tel Aviv in just a few short hours and the cold, pitiless truth was he didn't have a clue where to go from there.

What will happen once I get there? Should I call them or just leave things as they are and go back to my own life? Lord, I don't know what to do—I'm so confused.

Van Eaton longed to see his friends, and of course Peter, but he ached with the memory of his actions over the past two days. *But what about forgiveness? Isn't that the whole basis for my new life in Christ?* he asked himself. Truth be known, forgiveness was such a foreign sentiment that he was having a real problem coping with it—both giving and receiving, but especially the latter because it carried such a strange sense of obligation, at least that's how he perceived it. *But is penitence saying you're sorry and then simply forgetting about it? It just sounds too easy and it always has.*

His eyes glazed over in thought as he considered the writings of the Apostle Paul. *'What shall we say then? Shall we continue in sin that grace may abound? Certainly not! How shall we who died to sin live any longer in it?'*

"How shall we indeed?"

† † †

"He should've called by now," Elizabeth whispered. "I'm beginning to worry about him."

"Yeah me too," Paul said. "I can't imagine what has happened to cause him to act this way."

While they talked, Peter fiddled with Elizabeth's phone when it began to vibrate. He held it for a couple of cycles before handing it to her.

"It's Brad—he's a friend that's keeping my dog. I'm not going to say anything about what happened today." She took a deep breath and pressed the *answer* button.

"Brad… I'm doing well, how about you? Yes, I'm having a great time." There was a pause, then her eyes indicated what Paul had already expected. "Yes, we heard about it, but we were in no danger." She bit her lip, glaring wide-eyed at Paul.

"No, we're fine, but I'm glad you called, I've sort of had a change of plans." She scrunched her nose in anticipation. "I'm going to Baltimore." Another pause. "No, everything is fine. It's a special case… we'll be leaving here in the morning. Anyway, how's Winchester?" There was a ruffling over the phone. "Hey buddy… how's my boy huh?" she went on. "You think he knows it's me? Yeah? Good."

Brad waited for her to finish. "So you're going directly to Baltimore? I had hoped to talk to you when you got back. I ah, I have news too."

"What's that?"

"I… I really don't know how to say this, but—well, I've met

someone."

"Oh?"

"Yeah. I'm sorry Liz. It just happened." There was a long pause before he went on. "She's actually an old friend I dated in college and we happened to run into each other at lunch last week."

"And one thing led to another…" she said.

"Yeah I guess so. I'm sorry."

"It's okay Brad. I understand more than you may know."

"Thank you. But listen, I'll make sure Winchester is taken care of until you get home."

"I appreciate it," she said. "That means a lot. I'll touch base with you when we get to Baltimore."

"You sure you're okay?"

"It's fine Brad, really. No worries—bye now."

Elizabeth pressed the end button and for a moment replayed the call in her head. She actually didn't know whether to be hurt or relieved. *Ending relationships is always a difficult thing,* she thought, *but where one door closes—*

"Is everything all right?" Paul asked.

"Yeah, everything's fine," she smiled innocently. "Have you called home yet?"

† † †

"Operator, the country code is 001, and the area code is 901. Yes. 634— yes that's correct."

This was the call Paul had dreaded since they found out they were going to Mount Olive Medical, not to mention the explosion that was all over the news. He only hoped she'd understand.

"Hello? Laura?"

"Paul, are you all right? Did you hear about the bomb that went off?"

"Yes honey, we're fine… everything's fine. There's nothing to worry about." He pulled the phone away from his ear. "She heard."

"Was it close to you? Did you hear it when it went off?"

"Uh oh, another call is beeping in." Paul read the number. It was Van Eaton. "Hey honey, I need to call you back?"

"Are you sure you're all right?" she asked.

"Yes honey, everything's fine, I'll call you back."

THIRTY-EIGHT

Thursday afternoon, April 9

"Professor? Prof—hey, how are you brother?"

Elizabeth muted the TV.

"So how was your flight? Uh-huh. Well that's better than most," he laughed superficially. "Are you coming here? Mmmm hmmm, well you need to." Paul felt as if he was talking to a stranger.

"Listen to me. We're flying home tomorrow. We've all got seats on a private jet, including you if you want to come with us." There was a long pause. "Baltimore… to Mount Olive Medical Center. Elizabeth has it all set up." He waited. "Of course Peter is coming. He's the reason this all came together… yes."

"Tell him we all want him to come," Elizabeth whispered in.

Paul held up his hand in a wait-a-second gesture.

"Professor, we want you to come with us," he pressed. "We'll be the only ones on the plane. Uh-huh. I mean Baltimore is what, forty-five minutes from D.C.?"

Peter's eyes wandered the room while he listened, imagining the possibilities of such a device in his day.

"The plane will be at Ben Gurion in the morning," Paul went

on. "On the North end of the field… the Bedek Aero Center," he read from Elizabeth's notes. "We'll be there by eleven a.m. Yeah. Professor—it wouldn't be the same without you. You know you're a part of all this." A stony silence followed his comment.

Paul pulled the phone from his ear and laid it on the table.

"He just got off the plane in Tel Aviv. He's got a six-hour-layover."

"So is he coming?"

"I don't know, but it doesn't sound like it."

"So what do you think is wrong with him?"

Paul took a deep breath and let it out. "I don't know, but I'm really worried about him."

Peter hitched up his pants and came beside Paul. "We must pray for Pro-fes-sor Van-Ea-ton," he said, pronouncing every syllable of his name. "Will you join with me?"

"Your departure gate will be 'B' as in bravo, twenty-three," the gate attendant repeated, barely looking up from her screen. "Go to the end of the hallway and follow the signs to the 'B' gates. You have plenty of time, the flight has been delayed." She paused and gazed sympathetically at the professor. "Would you like for me to get you a shuttle?"

Van Eaton gathered his briefcase and overcoat. "I'll be fine."

Thirty-nine

Thursday evening, April 9

Paul dialed the number and waited for the phone to ring. *Am I ready for this?* he thought. *Maybe she's not home, maybe—*"Hey honey," he chirped, hoping to liven his tone. "I wanted to call you back before it got too late. How are you?" He stalled. "Uh huh, yeah—" He took a deep breath and sighed. "Listen, I need to tell you something, but I don't know exactly how to do it." He waited. "No, nothing's wrong… it's just that, well, something's come up— and I'm coming home tomorrow… well not home, but back to the states." Again he waited. "I wanted to tell you, but I didn't want to alarm you. No honey, everything's fine, it's just that—I didn't—I didn't know how—" A lengthy pause and Paul looked as if he was being read the riot act. "Laura, everything is fine, I promise. To Baltimore. Maryland. Yes, of course. I'll explain everything when I get stateside. I know it's a lot to ask, but please, just trust me, everything's fine honey I promise. I love you more than you'll ever know."

Paul pushed the end button and slid the phone into his pocket. "She's not a happy camper."

"We don't like to think we've been lied to," Elizabeth chided gently, siding with Laura as if it was her duty.

From across the room, Peter overheard Paul's conversation with his wife, his thoughts drifting to an exchange he'd once had with his own wife—

† † †

"I am to meet with Andrew in the morning," Peter sighed.

Abigail, already in bed, turned and met his gaze. "Your brother loves you Simon," she said.

Peter shot her a glance. "I know that Woman." Several uneasy moments passed. "He just needs to pay attention to his fishing and not chasing after every Rabbi with a story."

Abigail tucked a stray lock under her night-scarf and squinted through the shadows at her husband. "He is just high-spirited Simon, you know that."

Peter dropped his nightshirt over his head and tied the collar. "He is high-spirited Abigail—" He wanted to go on, but didn't.

"Just give him some time," she added.

Peter climbed into bed and pressed his finger to Abigail's lips. "You are beautiful," he doted. She touched him on the cheek, then folded her arms behind her head and focused on the ceiling. A cobweb fluttered. "You have been drinking again," she said matter-of-factly. "Maybe you should meet with that rabbi yourself."

Peter rolled to his side and sat up. "Are you going to tell me how to live my life now?"

Abigail sighed and extinguished the oil lamp. The room went black amid long heavy breaths. It was going to be a long night.

Forty

April 10, Good Friday a.m.

Paul tapped on Peter's door and it creaked open. Inside, Peter stood at the window, staring out at the morning sky tinted in soft pinks and blues though the sun had not yet penetrated the horizon. He was disheveled. He turned to Paul, pockets prevalent under his eyes, making him look much older than he was.

"He was crucified this day—" he said, his voice raspy with sleep.

Paul closed the door and sank to the edge of the bed. "Yes."

Peter drew a deep breath and turned back to the window. "Do you suppose that we will return to Israel?" he asked timidly, even childlike.

The question hung in the air as Paul came alongside the big fisherman. "I don't know, but I can tell you this, whatever happens, I'll be with you every step of the way. I can assure you of that."

Peter smiled briefly. "We followed the Master for nearly three seasons," he said dolefully. "And now, for Him not to be here is so strange."

Paul draped his arm around Peter and pulled him close. "I

don't know what to say, brother. But I know that you're here for a reason, just as we were in your time. And I can't tell you when… but you'll find out in God's time. I have no doubt of that."

Peter managed a weak smile.

"We were so bold when the Master was with us—the twelve of us. I was fearless then, as if there was nothing I could not do. But now that He is gone, I feel so alone… in here." He jabbed his chest as tears sprang to his eyes.

"I can only imagine," Paul said softly, "but that's where Jesus has been for my entire life—except for last week." Paul brought his palm to his own chest. "And it's been the same for every man, woman and child that has come to know Him since the resurrection. It's been totally by faith."

Peter cased the room for a moment, then brought his eyes back to Paul.

"I have never thought of it in that way," he admitted. "But you are right. Every generation since then, came to know the Master without the benefit of seeing His face… or hearing Him speak or touching his calloused hands." His words trailed for a moment. "Yet you still came to know Him."

"Yes. But it was because of you—and those who carried His story to the world." *No matter that Jesus hadn't even given the great commission at the time Peter had followed them into the future.*

"Would I even have the faith you possess had I not known Him as I did?" Peter mused. "And yet you believe—though until a week ago, you had never laid eyes upon Him. You truly believed by faith alone."

Then, as if on cue, the sun in all its splendor pierced the horizon and it was as if a revelation swept over Peter's soul. His eyes brightened and like the sun shone across the earth, a beatific smile spread across his face.

"Let us go to Amerika."

Forty-One

April 10, Good Friday a.m.

Two husky porters wrestled the bags out of the trunk and placed them on a cart as the entourage exited the limo. Paul stepped out first and helped Elizabeth. Peter slid to the edge of the seat, his gaze going past Elizabeth to a cluster of aircraft that were staged along a fence that bordered the airport. In that moment he wondered what this day would actually bring. He had become privy to so many astonishing revelations over the past week that he was almost numb. Almost. But now he was about to experience the technical advancement of the ages. Flight. It was something that those from his time would only dream about for another two millennia. And even though Paul and Elizabeth had tried to prepare him, there could be no adequate preparation.

Ben Gurion Airport was relatively quiet, at least this particular section of it. Paul was glad, but the armed guards at the entrance had a way of whisking him back to reality and it was obvious they had the same effect on Elizabeth. But this was the 21st century and their world as they had come to know it.

Entering the Bedek Aero Center, a representative from Mount

Olive stood with a hand-printed sign:

JONAH, STEWART, RYANN, VAN EATON.

Elizabeth pushed the strap on her backpack up to her neck and took the lead.

"Remember, just do what I do," Paul murmured. Peter nodded and followed, even aligning his steps with Paul's as they fell in behind Elizabeth.

"Your aircraft landed last night," the representative explained. "The pilots should be here within the hour though. They are planning on wheels-up by 13:30."

Peter's gaze shifted to the floor, he didn't even bother trying to understand what that meant.

Paul glanced at his watch. It was 11:05.

"And where is Mr. Van Eaton?" The man's words were curt, but polite.

Paul's smile faltered. "I guess he's not going to show. He may already be home for all we know. We'll keep our schedule, and if he's not here in time, we'll just have to go without him."

"That will not be a problem," said the representative. "Now, if you will follow me, I will walk you through customs." He gestured for them to move ahead as Israel's version of the TSA watched them closely.

Elizabeth heard her phone ping. It was David:

Dr. Bernstein
Message
Today 8:05 AM

Liz, I'm sorry I couldn't
be there to see u off this
morning, but I'm sure u
could see how short-staffed
we are.

I'll miss you, but I totally
understand.

Just wanted u to know
that I believe u are a part
of something that may be
bigger than even u know.

I think so too. God is
good.

Yes He is. I also wanted to
let you know that my voice
mailbox was full when I got
in this morning. One of them
was from Sealey Pharma.

UR kidding me.

No.

How do u think it got
out?

Don't know, but I knew it
would, just not this soon.

What now?

Just keep your circle
tight. Don't volunteer any
information about anything
unless you know for sure
who they are.

K. Thank you for
everything.

Believe me, it was...is...my
pleasure. And I hope it will
be sometime soon that we
see each other again.

Me too David. Me too.

Oh someone else called here
too. He didn't leave a name
or number but said he had to
meet with me asap. Said he
knew u and it had to do with
Peter. I had no choice but to
tell him yes. I'm supposed to
meet him in an hour. Do you
know who it is??

Not that I know of, but
I would be careful. We
met a man yesterday at
the Garden Tomb but
I don't know where he
went. He said he was the
curator but apparently
that wasn't the truth.

You were at the Garden
Tomb yesterday??

I'm sorry I didn't want u

to worry.

Well I would have.

See there! lol ☺

I'm serious Elizabeth. These
people can be ruthless.

I understand. Plz let me
know what u find out.

I will. Have a safe flight.

Talk soon?

You bet. Tonight soon enough?

I'll try to be patient. ☺

Forty-two

April 10, Good Friday

"So this is an *air-craft*?"

Elizabeth hid her grin. "Well, it's not like any aircraft I've ever been on, but yes." She stroked the polished burl counter that ran the length of the bulkhead, separating them from the forward cabin.

The posh interior of the Dassault Falcon 900 was even more luxurious than Peter anticipated. A veritable lair of opulence and comfort, down to the fully reclining, leather seats. Peter said in his land these were "such luxuries only kings were afforded." Paul had also explained to him back in the hotel that the pressure of the air in the cabin would change once they were in the air and that he would feel it, but not to be alarmed. *Alarmed?* Peter thought. Floating on air brought elation rather than alarm.

As Paul stepped inside, a man made his way from a forward cabin and extended his hand. "Mr. Jonah, I presume?"

Paul pointed to Peter.

"Ah, Shalom. I am Mordecai. I will be your host for the journey to our facility in Baltimore—"

Peter extended his hand as Paul had taught him and the two

men shook firmly.

Mordecai moved nimbly for such a wide man. His face was round and his eyes bulged, probably from a thyroid condition. His beard and mustache were salt and pepper, though mostly salt, and he was very business-like—dressed-to-kill so to speak. He wore a dark vested suit with a white button-down shirt and a steel gray tie, appearing much like Mr. French from the 1960's TV series *Family Affair*. He even flashed a gap-toothed smile that was warm and charming. He was a soft-spoken man, but his manner made it clear that he was in charge.

"I will also be your attaché for the duration of your stay at Mount Olive, Mr. Jonah. So if there is anything you need, please don't hesitate to let me know."

Peter looked at Paul who nodded gingerly. He mirrored his moves.

"You can sit wherever you like," Mordecai went on. "Our flight is scheduled to depart momentarily. We'll be in the air for approximately nine hours."

Paul flashed a smile and steered Peter toward a seat as they thanked him in unison.

† † †

The whine of the jet engines spooling up was unsettling to the apostle who had never heard such a resonance, ever. He clutched the armrests and squeezed as he sensed the pressure change.

"You okay?" Elizabeth's words carried a soothing maternal bent.

"I am good," he countered, albeit a little too quickly.

Elizabeth took him by the hand and stroked his wrist as Paul reached across the aisle and gave Peter's seatbelt a final tug.

"We will taxi out to the runway where we will fly off into the heavens," Elizabeth swept her hand forward in a flying gesture. "You're going to love this Peter, I guarantee it."

Peter managed a guarded smile.

Taxiing across the hot black tarmac, the plane unexpectedly slowed and ground to a whining halt. Mordecai unbuckled his belt as the captain stepped out. The two men spoke for a moment.

Mordecai came from the front cabin and motioned to Paul. "It appears as though we will have an additional passenger—" With effort he unlatched the door as the stairs folded out with a hiss and a limo pulled up to the plane. A surly figure ambled onto the tarmac and up the stairway, his hair tousled and his clothes not much better.

"Professor!" Elizabeth was out of her seat before she knew it along with Paul. Peter, not knowing how to free himself stayed put. "We thought you'd already gone back—" she confessed. She went to hug him, but he stiffened.

Paul shook Van's hand heavily, not really knowing where to begin or even if he should. "Well look what the cat dragged in," he said, attempting to lighten the mood.

"So professor, what do you think about all of this?" Elizabeth jumped in.

He flashed an obligatory smile. "It's very nice," he said as he gathered his belongings and with that all-too-recognizable smirk, made his way to a seat and plopped down.

Paul and Elizabeth's glances locked. The contemptable scholar had returned.

FORTY-THREE

April 10, Good Friday

"My ears pop as if I were climbing Mount Hermon," Peter chuckled to himself. He worked his jaw to free his eardrums, all the while glued to the window, mesmerized by the clouds rushing past as they climbed out over the azure blue waters of the Mediterranean. Above, the horizon curved gently, blending sky and sea into a soft gradient of blue that faded to pink.

Liz watched Peter as she reached into her bag for her phone. She looked at David's message and savored the moment. There was definitely something there if for no other reason than she craved more closeness to him. Thank goodness Brad had taken the first step in ending their relationship. Now she was guilt-free to pursue a connection to David. She smiled at just the moment Peter looked at her. He interpreted it as her sharing his delight.

Elizabeth now turned her focus to Peter, only imagining how he must feel about the goings on around him. He was literally being catapulted through the air faster than any human from his own time and it just added to the drama. And since it was almost too much for her to fathom, she only assumed that he would be dumbfounded all the more. But what about God the Father? What about His hand in all of this? Then, as she had done every single day, multiple times a day for the last two weeks, she reminded herself that God truly was in control.

A smile inched across her face as she spied a flight magazine. She pulled it from the seat pocket and, lowering the tray table, she flipped to the maps. She took a pen and traced a line from where they were to their destination.

"We're right here," she showed Peter, circling Israel. "We'll fly across the ocean more than six thousand miles to the United States—all the way over here to Baltimore Maryland."

"Mary-land?" Peter repeated.

"Yes. It is a state in the northeastern part of our country."

Peter took the map and studied the curvature of the diagram, then looked quizzically at Elizabeth. "The world is round?"

† † †

"I was surprised that the professor was able to get on the plane since we had already left the gate," Paul admitted to Mordecai. "I mean, don't get me wrong, I'm glad he's here, I just—"

Mordecai arched an eyebrow. "His name was still on the manifest which allowed him to be cleared through customs," he explained. "Though I must admit it's the first time I have ever seen it happen."

Paul got the pretext that Mordecai was annoyed that Van Eaton had joined them. Mordecai's nuanced attitude toward him seemed defensive, but he didn't know why.

From the rear of the plane, Paul watched the professor. It hadn't been that long since he'd watched him huff off and find another seat on their maiden flight to Israel, but surely that wouldn't happen again, not with everything they'd been through. Finally he unlatched his seatbelt and moved into the aisle. Glancing at Elizabeth he motioned toward Van Eaton. She nodded affirmingly.

"Is this seat taken?" Paul kept his tone lively.

Van Eaton zipped his bag shut and placed it on the floor as Paul slid in beside him.

"We've all been wondering when you were going to let us in on what was going on, professor."

Van Eaton superficially straightened his things, though he was careful not to make eye contact. He flipped through a magazine as if Paul wasn't even there.

If there was anything Paul had garnered from his life as a pastor, it was his training in clinical psychology. For this reason alone he knew not to press him.

Eventually Van Eaton closed the magazine and slid it into the seatback pocket. He propped his elbows on the armrests and laced his fingers together, resting his chin on his clasped hands. "I don't want to talk about it—" His voice carried a hint of cynicism.

"You know nothing could be so bad as—"

"I said—I don't want to talk about it!"

Paul eased back into his seat, ignoring his friend's tone. "Okay, brother. I'm here when you're ready."

Forty-Four
April 10, Good Friday

The vast expanse of the Atlantic appeared as blue veins shrouded in a field of soft cotton through the broken layer of clouds below. Peter pressed his face to the cold window, his breath fogging the glass. The low drone of the jet engines and the constant rush of air past the window was enough to lull one to sleep, unless of course, one had never witnessed such a sight.

"This is the view of angels," Peter murmured. He drew a long, deep breath and tried to take it all in, but it was almost too much to process… as if there was no room left in his brain. The whole idea of being on Earth more than twenty-one centuries after his own time, and the very fact that the date itself originated with the Master's birth, toyed with his already spinning head. At one point, he even speculated as to why Jesus hadn't chosen this time rather than his own.

With so many *creature comforts*, as Elizabeth had phrased it, why would one not choose this time in history to live? But there were inherent problems with this line of thinking as well, he reasoned. Jesus hadn't come to enjoy any such comfort man could offer. He came to earth literally to sacrifice Himself for all humanity, past present and future, all the while knowing this was the reason He came. He must have carried the burden of knowing His fate all along; and yet, He stayed the course, bearing the inexplicable heartache of knowing that He would die on a cruel cross.

And the real irony? The need for God in these modern, materialistic times paled in comparison with those of his own, simpler time, present company excluded. Paul and Elizabeth were two of the most Godly people he had ever come to know—and the professor too, though he had distanced himself since his return. He only hoped that whatever the reason, it would pass.

† † †

"What do you suppose has happened to the professor?"

Paul closed his Bible and straightened. "I don't know. I sat beside him for half an hour and he didn't say two words."

"I think we just need to give him some space. He'll come around." Elizabeth spoke, but was unconvinced.

"You know, even though he's a scholar, the professor is still a new believer," Paul stroked his Bible while he spoke. "There's no telling what he may have gotten himself into at that conference. And we both know that Satan would do anything to interfere with God's plans for Peter… and us too, for that matter."

Elizabeth sighed. "Yeah, yesterday at the tomb was about all the excitement I could stand for one day, but do you really think Satan has that kind of power over a believer?"

"Absolutely he does. Even though a person has surrendered to Christ and is truly regenerated, they can still fall. Coming to Christ doesn't stop temptation—or our inclination to sin."

"But, it's still 'once saved always saved', right?"

"What is this you are speaking of?" Peter overheard, seeming more curious than usual. After fumbling with the seatbelt he moved into the aisle, turning away from the window that had consumed almost every ounce of his attention since they had departed.

Paul straightened in his seat and measured his words. "It's nothing really—just one of those subjects that different religions debate. I guess that's why there are so many religions."

"Wouldn't Peter be the perfect one to ask about this?" Elizabeth asked. Her eyes danced from Paul to Peter and back.

Peter sat and listened without comment, not a trait that he was particularly used to, but he was doing his best to cultivate it.

"This was a discussion I was having with a pastor friend from a different faith the week before we left for Israel—" Paul explained. "And we were talking about the whole, *once-saved-always-saved* thing."

Peter wasn't about to interrupt now.

"So basically, it has to do with the conflicting views of Calvinist and Wesleyan doctrines. Wesley and Calvin were both preachers hundreds of years ago. Calvin lived about five hundred years ago and Wesley about three hundred. Calvin taught that once a person has committed his life to Christ, he is always saved, no matter what happens or what he does, hence the phrase, once saved always saved. He also taught election, but that'll be a discussion for another day. Anyway, the Wesleyan doctrine teaches that a person's actions *can* cause them to fall from grace and literally lose their salvation. But that's never made any sense to me. How can a person lose what is eternal?"

Peter smiled at them both with compassion. "Perhaps the emphasis should not be on *always,* but whether that person had truly committed his life to follow Jesus to begin with."

Paul nodded. "That's a valid point, but the question wasn't whether the person was a believer, but if a believer can sin and continue in sin. I think Wesleyans just can't accept the fact that people can still sin without losing their salvation."

Peter felt as if Paul's words reached in and touched his soul. It had been only days since he, by his own estimation had committed the most grievous of sins by denying he even knew Christ. And it was a wound that was still very fresh.

"But to what extent can a man sin?" Peter prodded further. "Are you implying a man can live a life of total disregard even though they have committed to follow Christ and His teachings?" *He wondered why he even posed such a question.* "Because in my estimation this would be an impossibility; commitment to Christ carries with it the highest accountability for all of our actions."

Paul nodded. "Yes, of course, the Apostle Paul talked about that in—well, I guess you really don't know about him yet."

Peter had no recollection of anyone named Paul other than pastor Ryann. Again he focused. "I remember the Master teaching that a tree is known by its fruit… that every good tree bears good fruit and bad trees produce bad fruit. But good trees don't produce bad fruit," he added. "Would this truth not tend to prove a man's relationship with God?"

"It should, but can a true believer choose to turn his back on God?" Paul treaded lightly.

Peter smiled at Paul's reasoning. "If you are asking can a follower of Christ stop following Him, I believe the answer is yes. In fact, there were many who came and went from our group over the years. Some stayed for days, and some weeks, but for one reason or another decided to leave or were pulled away for other reasons… family, occupation, we even had one young fellow who was so *homesick*, I believe that is what you call it, that he cried into the night, every night until finally we sent him home." Peter closed his eyes, trying to recall the boy's face. "And we never saw him again, but there were many like that. Do the Scriptures not tell of this story?"

Paul's face twisted into a grin. "The Scriptures say that there were so many stories about Jesus that there would not be enough books to hold them all."

"I can think of a few stories I hope never made it into the Scriptures."

Paul smiled and touched Peter's shoulder as empathy swelled

between them.

"But none of us knew for sure that Jesus was the Messiah," Peter went on. "Not until the night the Master revealed Himself to us. And after that night, no one left. In fact, no one would ever leave again, save Judas."

"So, once you all knew who Jesus truly was, it changed things?"

"Somehow I think we all knew, in here," he brought his hand to his chest. "But when Jesus finally confessed that He was the Christ, it was as if a breath of fresh air came over us all."

"And you were the first to claim that He was the Messiah," Paul asserted.

Peter looked strangely at Paul as if he was surprised that the pastor knew that. "Yes, I was the first—but I was also the first to deny Him."

An awkward moment came and went.

"As far as this question, once saved always saved, it sounds like both sides are basically saying the same thing," Elizabeth added. "A person who has truly committed their life to Christ will be a new creature, a good tree if you will. And just as Jesus said, 'a bad tree cannot produce good fruit.' So it appears that the real issue here is whether a true relationship with Christ has been established—and I think that is something only God can answer."

Peter watched Elizabeth closely. "You know, I remember John speaking of this subject not long ago," Peter said. "He always seemed to be very sensitive to the matter of relationships. I had hoped to talk with him further about it."

Elizabeth took Peter's hand and patted it. "I believe you will Peter. I truly believe you will."

FORTY-FIVE

April 10, Good Friday

Peter watched professor Van Eaton. The man he had known for little more than a week was troubled—there was no doubt. His actions were more than telling, even his mannerisms seemed to indicate that something was wrong.

People are the same, he thought. *Two thousand years later and they are still the same.* He bowed his head and whispered a silent prayer. Moments passed until he opened his eyes and caught Van Eaton looking at him. More minutes passed until Peter stood and made his way over.

"May I?"

Without comment, Van Eaton motioned for Peter to sit.

In the seats ahead, Paul and Elizabeth realized what was going on and both began to pray.

"You are hurting—" Peter said matter-of-factly. True to form, Peter jumped right into the situation. It was this trait Van Eaton identified with most.

Van Eaton blinked back tears. "Things… have happened… since I left you all last week," he admitted. "Things I'm not especially proud of."

Peter sat and listened, not saying a word as Van Eaton went on.

"I was to give a speech to my colleagues," he began, "at a yearly event that I have performed successfully for many years, but this year was so different—obviously."

Peter smiled thoughtfully.

"—And it wasn't so much what I said. I knew what I had to do and I felt like I did it, but I must admit it didn't turn out as I'd planned. And the repercussions that followed were even worse." His eyes wandered for a moment. "I may lose my position at the university," he sighed. "But even that doesn't concern me as much as my actions later that night." Tears spilled from his eyes as he considered the impact of his words.

"I—ended up in a situation with—" he paused long enough to confirm that Paul and Elizabeth were out of earshot. "With a woman."

Peter listened intently. He knew that Van Eaton was baring his soul and he didn't take that lightly.

"But it's not what you might think," Van Eaton clarified.

"I am thinking nothing other than my concern for you, dear friend."

Van Eaton smiled. "Of course. Well, ultimately nothing happened—not really, but it was foolhardy for the simple fact that I let it go that far. I had one of the most important nights of my life and it nearly ended in disaster. Then to top it off, I went back to my room and drowned my sorrows in a bottle."

Peter furrowed his brow.

"I got drunk."

Peter smiled reassuringly, as if he understood more than he let on.

"That is how the devil works," Peter said. "He prowls like a roaring lion, seeking whom he may devour. And he will go to great lengths to convince you that you are a lost cause."

"Tell me about it—"

Peter offered a slight nod. "I shared with Paul earlier that I was glad the Scriptures did not elaborate on every story that went into them—"

Van Eaton looked strangely at Peter. "O-kay."

"You see, Paul had shared with me only last night how the Scriptures spoke of me and my brother Andrew and the day Jesus called us to follow him. It was there at the Sea of Galilee. I remember as if it was yesterday—"

Peter settled back into his chair and closed his eyes. Taking long deep breaths, he combed his fingers through his hair. "Can you understand how extraordinary these words were for me to hear?" He brought his hands to his chest. "I am in the Scriptures," his voice quivered. "Jesus saw something in me… in both of us, Andrew and me, though sometimes I wonder what He truly saw."

Van Eaton smiled, knowing the only alternative would have been even more tears. *Peter's humility is always so purely innocent,* he thought.

"Andrew had been waiting on the shore for me to return that morning," Peter began. "I can still see his face as he pulled the empty boat to the shore. 'What, no catch?'" he asked. "I hadn't the heart to tell him I had not been fishing at all. What the scriptures fail to say is what I had been doing," He waited, weighing if he should continue at all. "Well—I had been drinking," he said as if he was relieved to share it.

Van's eyes shifted to meet his.

"Do not take me wrongly, I was not given to wine," he clarified. "Wine robs a man of reason as you well know. But I had faults… and I do still. James, John, all of us. But that night I had quarreled with my wife and left the house in a rage. Soon I found myself standing on the shore and decided to take the boat out. Eventually I drifted off to sleep and slept until the dawn. When I returned to the shore, Andrew was there waiting. Then not long after that we saw Jesus walking on the shore and He approached us. Can you imagine that?

I had spent the night in utter despair, but when the morning came, I met Jesus. And somehow I knew my life would never be the same again."

Van Eaton languished in a sea of emotions, not really knowing how to respond.

"And it all began with me drinking," Peter added.

"I guess God can use any event He chooses," Van Eaton spoke just above a whisper.

Peter nodded. "God takes us just as we are, He just doesn't leave us that way."

Van Eaton allowed the bittersweet reality to sink in. "No, I guess He doesn't."

Forty-six

April 10, Good Friday

Mordecai ducked through the door of the front cabin and sat down beside Paul. A moment later Paul motioned for Elizabeth.

"I thought this would be a good time to discuss the process regarding Mr. Jonah's admission into Mount Olive." Mordecai flipped through the paperwork. "It says here on the affidavit that you; Doctor Stewart are the responsible party," he piped in an officious tone.

"Yes, that is correct."

Mordecai glanced at Elizabeth over the top of his readers. "When we arrive in Baltimore tonight and pass through customs, there will be a car waiting for us at the main gate. I will accompany Mr. Jonah to the quarantine center at the hospital and you and your friends will be staying at the Hilton."

Elizabeth swapped looks with Paul.

"It's just protocol," Mordecai went on. "Tomorrow, Mr. Jonah should be available for visitors in the afternoon."

"But I have to stay with him," Elizabeth said. "Peter—Mr. Jonah has never been out of the country. I don't think—"

"I assure you he will be fine," Mordecai's voice carried a slight patronizing tone.

"But I don't understand, we were promised that we would be with him every step of the way," Paul asserted.

"Unfortunately, that won't be possible." Mordecai glanced at his phone and stood up. "Excuse me please."

He made his way to the front cabin while Elizabeth took the seat next to Paul. "I've got a strange feeling about that guy."

"Really?"

"Yes, don't you?"

Paul glanced back at Peter who was still sitting with Van Eaton. "Not really, but I'm not always the most observant person. At least that's what my wife says." He grinned.

"I'm serious Paul."

"Okay, I'm sorry. What makes you say that?"

"Did you see what was on his phone?"

"No what?"

"When he got that text, it looked like it said it was from Yousef."

Paul shrugged.

"That was the name of the curator at the Garden Tomb yesterday, remember?"

"Oh yeah."

Elizabeth slumped back into her seat. "There's something about that guy that isn't right."

"What, you think he doesn't have Peter's best interest at heart?"

"I don't know." There was a short silence. "Would God even allow that?"

Paul shrugged. "I don't know."

Forty-Seven

April 10, Good Friday

Professor Van Eaton unbuckled and stood with effort. Sitting with Peter for more than an hour had given him fresh perspective in many areas of his life and yet, he still seemed reticent, as if he was still holding on to something.

"You know," Peter began. "The night of the Passover meal the Master shared with me that Satan sought to sift me like wheat," he gave a side-glance and stroked his beard, recalling the night. "At first I thought, why me? But then I came to understand that Satan always stands against those God intends to use."

Van Eaton looked at Peter, blinking back the tears. "But I can't forget those things I've done."

Peter glanced at Van Eaton and went on. "We are all susceptible to his inducements brother, whether in my time or here in yours, things are no different. But we must understand that the sins we cannot forget, God cannot remember."

Van Eaton ran his rheumy fingers through his thinning hair. "I like that—but sometimes forgiveness is slow in coming… especially when we are trying to forgive ourselves."

Peter smiled reassuringly. "The Lord is not slow in keeping his promise as some understand slowness," he said. "But he is patient with you, not willing that any should perish, but that all should come to repentance."

Paul came beside Van Eaton in just enough time to hear Peter's words. He stared at the apostle in amazement. "That is virtually word for word what you will write in your second letter in the scriptures."

Peter didn't know how to respond.

"But you haven't—never mind."

† † †

Thumbing through a flight magazine, Elizabeth stopped at a picture of Times Square. "America won't be like anything you've ever seen before Peter." She handed him the magazine.

Peter took it and turned the picture ninety degrees, then back.

"So many people. What is this event?"

"It's no event," she explained. "It's twelve million people living together in the same place. It's called New York City."

"I have heard Rome to be this way," Peter said. "But I never imagined—"

"I guess Rome would be—or would have been much the same."

Peter fixated on the picture. He stroked the page as if it were three-dimensional. "This is where we are going," he said unequivocally. "To this *Time Square*."

"To Times Square? No, we're going to Baltimore," Elizabeth said.

Paul, half asleep, sat up straight in his chair. "What did he say?"

"He said we are going to New York."

"How would you know that Peter?"

The big fisherman shrugged. "I do not know."

FORTY-EIGHT

April 10, Good Friday

Peter watched in amazement as the sun slowly dissolved into the vast horizon. Now nearly six hours into the flight he was no more accustomed to the events that surrounded him than when they started, and perhaps even more perplexed.

"What is the—how do you say it—the tyme?"

Paul glanced at his watch and thought. "Well, its 8 o'clock in the evening from where we left Tel Aviv."

"So, it is Sabbat?"

"Well, yes, I suppose it is… there, but with the time change—" Paul thought for a moment. "Time change is a bit more complicated when you are flying."

Peter turned back to the window. "The Master taught us that Sabbat was made for man and not man for Sabbat." He smiled thinly, finding irony in his words. "I used it as an excuse more than I should I suppose."

Paul listened as Peter reminisced. He could only imagine how Peter felt.

"All of the things that are going on around you have got to

be so unbelievable to you Peter." Paul chose his words carefully. "Not that our journey to your time wasn't truly amazing as well, but we had an idea of what was going to happen just from knowing the scriptures. But you don't have any of that to guide you through what is happening here. Or us for that matter, but at least we're in our own time."

Peter listened without comment.

"But sometimes it plays with my head. I mean you are Simon Peter, here with us in the 21st century, and yet you lived two thousand—"

Peter held up his hand, "I have come to terms with the fact that there are things I must know nothing of…" he said.

Paul gripped Peter's shoulder. "You're right brother, I don't know what I was thinking. I'm sorry."

Peter placed his hand over Paul's and smiled, his worry dissolving into a tentative smile. "I do not know what is to come, but I am confident the Father does, and that is enough for me."

Paul smiled. "And me."

Mordecai stood in the shadows of the galley just within earshot, his mouth twisting into a maniacal grin.

Forty-nine

April 10, Good Friday, P.M.

"Falcon 900, November one-zero-niner-alpha-tango, I have an amendment to your route. Advise when ready to copy."

"Niner-alpha-tango, go ahead."

"November niner-alpha-tango, in twenty miles join Victor 145 inbound to the St. John's vortac. Take the Kennedy Seven Arrival into LaGuardia."

"LaGuardia?" Captain Lynn Holmes' Adam's apple rose and settled against the knot in his tie. "What's going on?" he looked at his second officer.

"LaGuardia approach, Dassault Falcon niner-alpha-tango, we are filed for Baltimore Washington, sir."

"Niner-alpha-tango affirmative, but this front moving in has brought ceilings down to zero up and down the seaboard from as far south as Charleston up as far north as Logan."

"What about Philly or Dulles?"

"All zero-zero."

"And LaGuardia is still open?"

"For now, yes sir. I need you to expedite your descent, we're starting to back up."

Captain Holmes settled back in his chair as the second officer dialed in the new coordinates. The aircraft banked gently right then leveled out. "Can you believe that? I can't say I've ever seen LaGuardia open and everybody else down."

"I haven't either. Ever."

† † †

Captain Holmes stooped and stepped out of the cockpit. He glanced at his watch and shook his wrist. "Well folks, a slight change of plans—" his tone was level and calm. He leaned over the first row of seats and glanced at Mordecai. "It's looks like we won't make it into Baltimore tonight. A front is moving up the Eastern Seaboard that's got everything shut down. So it looks like we're going to have to—"

Paul sat up and wiped the sleep out of his eyes. "Where are we?"

"Well, that's the thing. We just passed Boston Logan… and they're directing us into LaGuardia."

"New York?" Elizabeth didn't even try to stifle her grin.

"That's the place, and there's a nice FBO there on the field that offers amenities for passengers and pilots." He smoothed his tie as he spoke. "We should be on the ground in about an hour."

Elizabeth and Paul both turned their attention to Peter. His 'I told you so' expression was priceless.

Fifty

April 10, Good Friday, P.M.

A canopy of thick clouds gathered low over the Manhattan skyline, reflecting a pale hue from the lights below as the aircraft made its turn onto final approach. Peter was glued to the window. He pressed his face against the cold glass as the plane dipped in and out of the clouds, forming tiny streams of water that streaked past each window.

As they waited to descend, Mordecai huddled in a corner of the galley. He had one bar on his phone, but it was enough of a signal to make a call. He punched in the numbers.

"There's been a change of plans," he whispered. "We've been diverted to New York." There was a long pause. "Where is that worthless heathen who was supposed to make everything run so smoothly?"

The question hung in the air for a moment.

"Ridiculous!" Mordecai said. "Get him to the city! How did I come to place you in a position of such importance in my organization? Perhaps I was wrong to have assumed you were up to the task." He ended the call, seething.

† † †

Elizabeth watched Peter. The man she had come to know and revere as an apostle of Christ was, in this instance, more like a child. She couldn't have peeled him from that window had she wanted to. His eyes were wide and bright, taking in sights that would mesmerize anyone who witnessed them for the first time.

An endless sea of lights varying in size, color and quantity peppered the landscape in every direction as far as Peter could see. With every street, a perfect row of lights defined the roadways that divided city blocks. And the traffic! It was as if there were a million moving strings of stars, flickering lights from as far as the Brooklyn and Manhattan Bridges on the East river to Queens and the Bronx on the West Side. But Peter was privy to none of that. He no more knew where he was than a child who had lost his parents in a large crowd.

He jumped as the landing gear rattled the fuselage and cycled down into place. The wind whistled noticeably over the din in the cabin as the landing gear and flaps resisted the airflow, slowing them down in the process.

With a jolt they touched down and made the first turnoff, falling in behind a tug that led them to the FBO. As the engines spooled down, Mordecai unbuckled and went to Paul.

"I've arranged for a limousine to meet us outside once we are cleared through customs. We'll be staying at the Waldorf." He paused as Paul swapped glances with Elizabeth. Mordecai glanced over the top of his glasses. "We are Mount Olive after all," he asserted, then he lowered his voice. "Once we are checked in, should you decide to venture out, I cannot stress the importance of keeping Mr. Jonah with you at all times. Mount Olive has spared no expense to retain Mr. Jonah's—ah, endowments and it is my responsibility to see that he makes it to Baltimore safe and sound."

"It shouldn't be a problem," Paul assured.

Elizabeth agreed and went to Peter who was still in his seat.

"I need you to do something," she hinted. She shrugged off her backpack and pulled out a surgical mask. "I need you to wear this."

She took the mask and draped the elastic strips around Peter's ears. "I want you to keep this on until we're out of the airport."

Peter pressed the mask against his face and looked strangely at her.

"Trust me," she said with a wink.

† † †

Elizabeth gathered her things as a text dinged her phone. It was Ray Roaten.

Dir. Ray Roaten
Message
Today 7:05 PM

Elizabeth, this is Ray, have
you landed?

> Yes, we just touched
> down. How are you?

I'm okay, but I have some
disturbing news. I'm sorry to
have to tell you but we just
received word that Dr.
Bernstein was shot in his
office today.

> Oh my God is he all
> right?

They said he's in ICU and
they have their best
team working on him.

What happened Ray?

Reports are sketchy, but
they said he was supposed
to meet some guy and
the next thing they heard
gunshots from his office and
the guy ran out the ER exit.
The cops are all over this
looking for him.

Please keep me posted
and know that I'm
praying for him.

Absolutely.

FIFTY-ONE

April 10, Good Friday, P.M.

Elizabeth stepped down onto the tarmac, her stomach in knots. Even though she had only known David for a short time, she had a strong connection with him. The news shook her to her core.

And what could have happened? He didn't just have a stroke or a heart attack, he was shot! *Could I have had something to do with it? Or Peter?* Her head was exploding with notions, but she knew she had to stay calm.

† † †

"Are you coming Liz?" Paul was already holding the door to the customs entrance.

Elizabeth painted a compulsory smile that did not reach her eyes. *All things work together for good—*she thought. *All things.* It was a verse she'd taken to heart during her second tour in Iraq after losing two of her close friends… one while still in her arms.

"Yes! Coming!"

Fifty-two

April 10, Good Friday, P.M.

The first apostle to ever set foot on American soil waited anxiously in the nine by five cubicle. Customs agent Daniel Holyfield sat directly across from him, posing the usual questions and watching for any telltale signs that might signal suspicion. He flipped through Peter's paperwork.

Holyfield instantly profiled Peter. And how could he not? He had the look, as if the black scraggly beard and his deep, olive complexion weren't telling enough. He struggled not to pass judgment.

"Mr. Jonah, it says here that you are an Israeli national?" Flecks of spittle sprayed from his mouth as he spoke.

Peter swallowed hard.

"And where are you from originally?"

"My home is Capernaum. I was born there."

"Uh, huh. And why are you traveling to the United States?"

Peter pulled his mask under his nose and glanced back over his shoulder. "Where are my friends?"

"They're close by. Just answer the question please."

Peter picked at his cuticles… and prayed.

The agent went on. "It says here that you are traveling on a medical visa."

"Yes."

"And what is your medical situation?"

"I cannot say."

"What?"

"I cannot say."

"And why is that?"

"Because I do not know."

Peter flinched as a hand fell heavily on his shoulder.

"Elizabeth. I thought you would never—"

"Peter you've got to keep your mask over your nose!" Elizabeth feigned surprise, but Peter wasn't catching on.

"I'm Doctor Elizabeth Stewart." Elizabeth extended her hand. "Mr. Jonah is under my care, Mr.— " She glanced at his nametag, "Holyfield."

"I need to let you know that the CDC has cleared Mr. Jonah to the United States, but I am not at liberty to confirm or deny that his condition is non- contagious." She was glad her mask concealed her grin.

The young customs agent thought for a moment, then abruptly stamped Peter's paperwork and handed it to Elizabeth, unwittingly wiping his hands on his pants.

Elizabeth led Peter into the hallway. "Let's get out of here."

FIFTY-THREE

April 10, Good Friday, P.M.

The air was thick with a medley of horns, screeching tires, and voices—all dissolving into the drone of the inner city. New York City. And people were everywhere—a sea of faces entwined with the sights and sounds that declared its namesake; the city that never sleeps. To the visitor it was truly entertaining. To the New Yorker, it was just another day. But to Peter, it was hypnotic.

As with the plane, Peter's face was pressed against the limo window, his breath fogging the glass. The artificial lights of the city seemed so strange to him. Never had he witnessed such bright acuity under the darkness of night. And the wondrous experiences never seemed to end.

"So this is New York…"

† † †

"We will plan to meet here in the lobby precisely at 6:00 a.m.," Mordecai spoke with a voice that was all business. "I plan to be up for a while should you need anything… and please, I cannot stress—"

"Yes, we'll take good care of Mr. Jonah," Elizabeth snapped, mentally chiding herself, still reckoning with the news of David's situation.

Mordecai motioned to the concierge and strode with effort to the elevator.

† † †

Paul plucked a few business cards from the concierge's lectern and handed them to Liz and Van Eaton. Even Peter took one for curiosity sake, not that he could read it anyway. He squirreled it away in his pocket.

"I was thinking about dropping our things off in the room and getting out for some fresh air," Paul said. "To clear my head. You guys want to come?"

FIFTY-FOUR

April 10, Good Friday, P.M.

The gilded mahogany revolving doors of the stately Waldorf Astoria were just one more chapter in a litany of innovations at which Peter marveled. Successfully passing through them carried its own experience as well.

Outside, beams of moonlight quietly pierced the clouds and washed over them. Even with the lights of the city, the moon was as large and luminous as they had ever seen it. And other than a contrail that scarred the clearing night sky, they would have thought they were all back in Jesus' time. Peter especially felt it, his mind drifting…

† † †

Standing timidly by the fire, Peter extended his palms toward the crackling blaze.

"The fire is good, no?" He spoke to someone, but he couldn't remember who it was.

"It doesn't matter—" a woman chided irritably. "The fact remains that the Sanhedrin has called a special meeting all because of Him. I always wondered what the real story was there. Miracles. Raising people from the dead! I knew it couldn't be true."

She turned toward Peter who edged toward the shadows.

"What is this? I know you! You are one of His disciples!" She grabbed for his arm, but he moved out of reach.

"What are you saying woman?" Peter's voice broke.

"He is a friend of the Nazarene. I am certain of it," another accused.

Peter's heart pounded at the accusations. "No! It is a lie!" He swore repeatedly. "I don't know the man do you hear me? I don't know Him!"

It was then, from across the courtyard, an entourage of temple guards spilled into the street, dragging a man, hunched over and shackled, stumbling along and struggling to keep up.

Peter froze when Jesus found him in the crowd and their eyes met. The wary disciple tried to look away—he even wanted to, but he couldn't. Instantly the angry mob thickened around Jesus, albeit half of them didn't even know what they were doing or why. The night was so electric with accusations that virtually everyone was anxious to come to blows. In all the confusion, Peter fled into the night.

Fifty-Five

April 10, Good Friday, P.M.

What began as a fifteen-minute jaunt to Times Square according to Paul's smartphone, turned into an expedition of detours through construction sites and backstreets… and not exactly through the best part of town. As the four made their way down a pot-holed street, they came to a long stairway that descended into a wide hallway awash in ashen light. The subway. Paul took the lead.

"C'mon, let's see if we can take the subway to Times Square."

† † †

After purchasing tickets, the four of them passed through the turnstiles and toward the gate. As late as it was, only a handful of people were waiting. Most of them were glued to their cellphones, but you could tell that they were very aware of their surroundings. New Yorkers always were. They had to be.

While the three batted around ideas the subway train slowed and screeched to a stop. The last of the regulars filed out and Peter, fascinated with the mechanics of the pneumatic door, stepped onto the car unnoticed. Then, without warning the doors hissed shut and the train began to move. Peter pounded on the glass, but there was nothing any of them could do. Paul came alongside the train as it pulled away, yelling at Peter. "Get off at the next stop and wait for us there! Okay? Just wait for us there!" He wondered if Peter had heard and understood anything he'd said.

For a moment everything was a blur. Then Elizabeth ran to the graphic on the wall and pointed to a green dot on the faded map. "We're here," she said. Her finger traced the line to the next stop. "This is the #6 subway. The next stop is 51st street—"

The three bolted up the stairs and spied a police officer on the corner.

"Where is the subway on 51st street?"

The officer backed up and took in the three.

"What?"

"The subway! Where is the entrance on 51st?"

"It's three blocks straight up that way but—"

"What? What?" Elizabeth was frantic.

"It's blocked off for repairs. You'll have to go to 55th."

Paul thanked the cop and ran to the curb, hailing a cab as Van Eaton slowly followed, his legs wobbling with exhaustion.

"Fifty-fifth!"

"Fifty-fifth and—" the driver repeated.

"Hudson," Elizabeth chimed in. "Please hurry!"

With barely a nod the driver wheeled the yellow Crown Vic into the traffic and buried the accelerator. Paul glanced at Elizabeth, remembering the first cab ride they'd shared in Jerusalem. Both scrambled for their seatbelts.

"I'm glad you had the foresight to give him a wallet with his I.D. at the hotel," Van Eaton said, his voice hoarse.

"He's got his wallet, but that's all he's got. He's no more going to know what to do than the man in the moon."

Fifty-six

April 10, Good Friday, P.M.

"Sir! We have a problem."

"I'm listening," said Mordecai.

"They've lost him—"

An awkward silence followed his remark.

"Jonah! They've lost Mr. Jonah!"

"What? Where are you?"

"I'm at the 51st street subway."

"Did they see you?"

"No, of course not."

"Well, I'm waiting to hear what happened."

"They were all talking and Jonah somehow ended up on the train—" The man stopped long enough to see if anyone was around him. "And the doors closed before anyone could stop them."

"Where are they now?"

"They hailed a cab and I heard them say they were headed to 55th."

"Then get over there and be quick about it! Call me when you know something!"

Mordecai slammed his phone on the nightstand, shattering the face.

"Imbecile."

FIFTY-SEVEN

April 10, Good Friday, P.M.

Peter gripped the cold, smooth, handrail with both hands as the train swept down the track toward the next stop. Fortunately, there were only a few patrons on his car at such a late hour, and none of them seemed to take notice of him. Finally the train slowed and ground to a halt. He recoiled instantly as the doors hissed and sprang open. Unenthusiastically, he stepped through the door and onto the platform while the indiscriminate passengers brushed past him and exited the station. He stood in silence as he watched the train lumber away and dissolve into the darkness.

He looked around. The room, awash with cobwebbed fluorescent fixtures, was cold and dank and smelled of urine. The floor that once must have been many shades lighter was filthy, even by his standards. And the mismatched tile that clad the walls was scarred with strange hieroglyphics he'd heard his friends refer to as graf-eet-ee.

But where were his friends now? For a moment he panicked as he came to grips with the inevitability that he was alone in a city of… what did Elizabeth say? Twelve million people. Twelve million. It wasn't even a fathomable number, but at this point it really didn't matter. Faith was beginning to take a stronghold, even though it was birthed out of necessity.

As he watched the last person ascend the long stairway and disappear over the top, he pulled his collar tight to his throat and sank his hands deep into his pockets. His breath fogged the air as he considered his next move. *If I stay, they may never find me, but if I go, I may find them. Yes, I must somehow find them.*

The cold night air whipped through the street as a cabbie laid on his horn and zipped past. Peter jumped back on the curb, a cold shiver reaching to his bones. He had known cold, but never like this. Thankfully, he'd listened to Paul and donned a pair of socks with his sandals before leaving the hotel. Now he would give anything to know where his friends were.

Father, I pray for guidance, casting all my care upon you—

Farther down the street, he caught a glimpse of a silhouette. The gauzy image crossed the street and joined others. They huddled for a moment then started toward him, Peter turned and hurried in the other direction.

As he walked, he remembered having his own share of scraps over the years, especially in his early years, and he still possessed good street-sense. It was one of those things he never completely forgot and he was glad of it.

Over the sound of his own footsteps, he could also hear the banter, though their language was a little more challenging to understand.

"Este Gringo…" Peter couldn't understand all of what they were saying, but enough to give him a sense that they meant him harm.

"Sup homey?" The words echoed off of a string of boarded-up storefronts lining the street on his right. He hurried further ahead.

"Hey rag-head, you deaf or something?"

Just ahead, a narrow alley appeared between two decrepit buildings. He ducked in and hurried down to the end but there was no exit. His heart pounded. Drawing short, sequential breaths he tried not to fog the air as he backed into the shadows. The darkness engulfed him. For a moment he felt safe as he whispered a silent prayer and waited. A minute later the four men followed.

"What are you doing on our turf old man?" The men, or boys as they were, surrounded him now. "Hey! We're talkin' to you old man!"

Peter didn't respond.

Then one of the men came forward and pressed a cold steel barrel—he only assumed it was a weapon—against his middle. "What you got in your pockets Gringo?" The man's nostrils glistened with white powder as he spoke. He blurted a few more expletives Peter assumed were profanities. For a moment he wished for the sword he'd brandished in the garden the night he'd taken off the chief priest's ear.

Peter tried to brace for attack, but a deafening blast was followed by something ripping through his gut. Instantly his face turned ashen and a wave of nausea washed over him. He grabbed his stomach with both hands, shaking uncontrollably as he stared into the man's acne-pocked face—as if asking why. Then he felt a sharp tightening of his abdomen. Searing heat filled the entry wound as the slug slowly pushed back out through the hole in his skin and fell to the ground. In an instant the wound closed and his skin fused together.

Peter's eyes inched back up to the men, whose faces were instantly washed in a brilliant light. He turned to see the seraph, Manasseh—sword drawn and hovering just behind and above him. When he turned back around the men were nowhere to be found.

FIFTY-EIGHT

April 10, Good Friday, P.M.

The light vanished as quickly as it had appeared. Peter stood in the darkness, waiting for his pupils to dilate.

In a moment the seraph took on human form and came to Peter. "The danger has passed," she assured.

Peter glanced over his shoulder. "I am glad you are so confident."

Manasseh smiled knowingly. "God never promised life without adversity," she said. "Moreover, it has always been the catalyst for growth."

Peter stroked his abdomen, but felt no pain from a scarless wound. "So you tarried on purpose?"

The seraph deflected the question. "There is a church," she went on, "less than a league from here—the church of the patron Saint Patrick. There you will meet a man—"

Peter smoothed his beard as he studied the seraph's face. "How will I know this man?"

"You will know."

"And what of my friends?"

The seraph's eyes wandered for a moment. "They will be along…"

Fifty-nine

April 11, Saturday

"He's not here!" Paul snapped. "How could I have been so stupid? I took my eyes off of him for one second and now this!"

"Don't beat yourself up Paul," Elizabeth insisted. "All three of us were there. Any one of us should've seen what was happening."

"She's right brother," Van Eaton chimed in. He slipped his hands into his pockets and thought for a moment. "You know the irony is that only a few hours ago, Peter told me on the plane that God could use whatever circumstances *He* chooses." He shook his head at the thought. "I hope he truly took those words to heart."

"Yeah, but what are we supposed to do in the meantime?" Paul spoke more to himself than directly to the professor.

"Maybe we don't need to do anything yet," Elizabeth suggested. She spied a coffee house just up the street. "Let's go in and get warm—clear our heads like we started out when we left the hotel?"

Just as Paul traded glances with Van Eaton his phone rang. He looked at the face and showed it to Elizabeth. It was Mordecai.

"Don't answer it," she said. "Not yet."

"Yeah, you're probably right."
"Just let it go to voicemail. We'll deal with it later."
Van Eaton massaged his temples… and prayed.

Sixty

April 11, Saturday, A.M.

The alley was still… almost too still. In the quiet of the moment, a cat leapt from a trashcan and flipped the lid into the street, cutting the night air like the crash of a cymbal. Peter sucked in a deep breath and quivered as he let it out. *My mission has been sanctioned by God,* he reminded himself. *I have no reason to fear. But how could I have stepped onto that…* sub—way *and become separated from my friends?* He brushed away the thought as he caught sight of another figure, this one not so challenging. He shambled toward Peter, turning up his bottle and swigging the last swallow. He flung it at a brick wall and it exploded into a million snowflake fragments. Clad in a soiled Army surplus jacket with tattered lapels, he staggered around Peter, making a full circle.

"This is my alley!" His words were slurred and rang hollow, his voice raspy with phlegm. Peter unconsciously drew back as the man edged closer. The stench of alcohol was strong, but not altogether foreign. Peter had dealt with more than his share of drunks in his own time—even in his own family.

"Sir, I have no quarrel with you," Peter said. "It is my

unfortunate plight to be here at all."

The old man purged his nostrils on the sidewalk and smeared the excess on his coat sleeve. Through the dim light, Peter watched him move. His body language aside, his whispering voice alone hinted that he was harmless.

"So, what are you doing here?"

The apostle considered a plausible response. "I ah, I do not know exactly." *No sense in lying,* he thought.

"You ain't no preacher are ya?"

Peter frowned.

"Yeah you are. You come here to save me preacher?" The man's eyes glistened in the darkness, his words full of desperation.

"Your answer is not in strong drink friend," Peter chided gently. It felt good to speak his heart.

The old man hocked and spit on the ground. "Why don't you go on back to your fancy cathedral and leave me be!"

Cathedral? Peter wished he fully grasped the English language.

"And where would that be?" he asked.

"You think I don't know where you came from?" He pointed up the street. "Right up there. Yeah, didn't think I knowed where St. Patrick's was, did ya?"

Peter turned and hurried up the street, suddenly realizing that was where he was supposed to go, but then he stopped. He turned and smiled at the man. "Strong drink is not the answer friend." He paused long enough for his words to take hold. "Your answer is in Christ. Only He can break those chains."

For a brief moment the man considered Peter's words. But then, as with so many times before, he wiped the tears from his face and his voice thickened with emotion. "I don't care if it hair-lips Hell and breaks the plan of salvation, I'm going to get another drink, you hear me preacher? I'm going to get another drink!"

Peter turned and walked away without saying a word, knowing all too well the grip that spirits could have on a man.

Sixty-One
April 11, Saturday, A.M.

The man with fingerless gloves ground a cigarette out on his shoe and stepped back into the shadows. Sporting a formidable frame, he was just over six feet and was inked and pierced, but done so in a tasteful way, if there could be such a thing. He pulled out his phone and punched in the numbers.

"I have eyes on them sir. They just went into a coffee shop."

"And Jonah?"

"Nothing yet, but—" He could sense Mordecai's disdain even over the phone. "But we will find him—I pledge my life on it."

Mordecai's eyes narrowed in an impish sort of way as he pressed the end button. *You may indeed.*

† † †

Paul warmed his hand on the cup while he stirred in creamer. "Don't worry, we'll find him."

Elizabeth managed a tight-lipped smile, then gazed at the floor. "I know, I'm just—I'm sorry."

"What would you be sorry for?"

Elizabeth looked at them pleadingly. "I need to share something with you—with both of you, but I don't know if this is the right time—"

"What is it?"

"It's about my contact in Jerusalem… Dr. Bernstein—" Her eyes swept the room. "He—he was shot yesterday. And he's in critical condition."

Paul exchanged stricken looks with Van Eaton.

"Oh Liz, I'm so sorry…" Paul took Elizabeth's hand and Van Eaton covered Paul's. "Why didn't you tell us?"

"I just found out when we landed," she said. "Ray Roaten—my boss, sent me a text." Tears pooled in the young doctor's eyes as she went on. "And there's something else," she said, choosing her words carefully. "I think the man from the Garden Tomb—Yousef might have had something to do with it."

"Why do you say that?"

"David—ah, Dr. Bernstein said someone that knew me contacted him yesterday and needed to meet with him, and I'm thinking it might be the same guy. Then I told you I thought I saw his name come up on Mordecai's phone when we were on the plane."

"You thought you saw? Are you sure?"

"Yes, that was the name I saw. I'm sure of it," she said, scolding him with an angry glare.

Paul saw that he struck a nerve. He pushed back from the table for a moment, lost in the thought. "Then that would implicate Mordecai as well."

A stony silence fell between the three.

"Then we've got to find Peter," Elizabeth confessed, standing up. "And we've got to find him now—it's going to be light soon."

Sixty-two

April 11, Saturday, A.M.

Eyes sparkling with anticipation, Peter followed the vast, angular structure looming against thick gray clouds scudded above. Then as if on cue, the clouds parted and the morning sun broke through in all of its glory. Peter instantly knew this was where he was supposed to be.

With effort, he pulled the hefty entrance doors apart and stepped into the foyer. It was empty, but warm, and a welcome change from the unseasonable cold that had taunted his bones for most of the night. That, and the nagging jet-lag, a factor he didn't fully comprehend, had also begun to take its toll. But rest was the furthest thing from his mind at this point. In fact, it was now abundantly clear that he was exactly where he was supposed to be— an incredible mission that he was undoubtedly destined for. And he wasn't about to slow down now.

Inside, mirror-polished marble floors shimmered with the smoothness of pure silk, reminding Peter of when he floated on a perfectly still Galilean Sea. And the morning sun, piercing the stained glass, painted rainbows across thick, polished oak pews.

Rows and rows were perfectly spaced, lining both sides of the vast cathedral. Peter had never witnessed such majesty or opulence in all of his life.

In the quiet of the moment, a figure entered from the front of the church holding something in his hands. He stooped and placed it on the floor, then gestured for Peter. Even at that distance, Peter could see the man carried such an air of splendor and sincerity that he knew he could be trusted. The weary apostle made his way down the long, center aisle with deference until he reached the front.

"Please come closer," the man's soothing tone put Peter even more at ease.

Now the big fisherman stood directly in front of the man he assumed to be clergy, but his visceral intuition indicated something more—even supernatural.

The priest brought his hand to his chest and bowed. "May I?" His voice was filled with emotion. Peter gently nodded consent. The man then lowered himself to the floor and removed an ornate scarf, revealing a metal basin of water. He took the scarf and folded it in half, then in half again.

Peter watched his every move without comment.

Now the priest gently took Peter by the ankle and loosened his sandal. He removed his sock and guided his foot into the bowl while Peter steadied himself on the pew beside him. With tears sliding down his cheeks, the clergyman went on to perform the servant's rite, scrupulously washing Peter's feet. Then as he finished, he carefully dried them and replaced his sandals. Quietly he stood.

"You… you are Peter, the rock," he said, his voice thickened with emotion. For a moment Peter was caught off guard, but then as the spirit revealed, his face dissolved to a tentative smile.

"I am."

Sixty-three

April 11, Saturday, A.M.

Paul downed the last of a lukewarm coffee and settled back into his chair. "If Mordecai is involved in Bernstein's murder attempt we're going to have to go to the police," he said.

"Or the F.B.I.—" Van Eaton added. "This is international."

"Worse than that, if he's involved with the attack on David, does it have something to do with Peter?" Elizabeth's heart skipped a beat. "Dear God."

Paul absorbed the comment. "We're going to have to get help, but I really don't know who we can trust."

"You know we've talked about this before, but would God even allow such a thing to happen to Peter?" Elizabeth asked. She drummed her fingers nervously as if she questioned her own sanity, her eyes darting from Paul to Van Eaton and back. "Do you think something has already happened to him?" She struggled to keep her voice level.

Paul shook his head at the thought. *Would God allow something bad to happen?* It was the same question he'd posed to himself a thousand times over the past two weeks and there seemed to be no definitive answer. And what made matters worse, God seemed to have become strangely silent.

Sixty-Four
April 11, Saturday, A.M.

The cathedral was perfectly still, and other than the occasional pops and creaks from the expansion and contraction of wooden pews, it was pin-drop quiet. The two men stood in silence, sensing an air of incredulity.

"I am *Monsignor*—" he corrected with a modest inflection. "*Joseph Sergetti.*" He motioned for Peter to sit as he sank to the pew and removed his zucchetto cap, placing it on the seat beside him. "I hardly know where to begin," he admitted. *I have a thousand questions, and a thousand more after that*, he thought.

Peter exchanged a meaningful gaze with the priest, choosing his words carefully. "The last person to wash my feet—was the Master himself," he said. Chill bumps coated the priest's arms. He neither knew how to respond or even if he should.

"I must ask, how is it that you know—what I mean to say is—" Peter grappled with his words.

"How do I know you are who you claim to be?" Sergetti clarified.

Peter nodded gently.

Sergetti's eyes sparkled. "Our Father has spoken to me through my prayers this entire week. And the moment you entered the cathedral, I knew. Even the water in this basin has been in here all week."

Peter rubbed his feet and smiled. "Yes—it was quite cold."

Both men dissolved to laughter as Sergetti inched closer to the big fisherman, his eyes again pooling with tears. "I'm sorry, it's just that, you are—you are Simon Peter, here in my very presence. I am so unworthy." He paused, then he quietly slid from the pew to the floor and knelt at Peter's feet. Struggling to keep his composure, he cupped his hands over his face as tears poured through his fingers.

Peter placed his hand on Sergetti's head and stroked his hair. "We are all unworthy," Peter said. "Do you not think that my denial of Him weighs on me still?" Peter spoke assuming Sergetti knew to what he was referring.

The priest wiped his eyes and looked directly at the apostle. "Yes, you failed Him, but no more than any of us on a daily basis," he countered. "And you will go on to—to live your entire life serving Him. Or you did." Sergetti looked strangely at Peter. "This is all so much to take in."

Peter helped the older man back to the pew.

Monsignor Joseph Sergetti was perhaps in his late sixties Peter assumed, but he could have been older. His dark hair was dusted with gray and lay in waves over his head. He moved slowly, but deliberately, carrying himself with the finesse of a man much younger in years. He was clean-shaven and scrupulously groomed, except for his bushy eyebrows that rose and fell as he spoke.

His devotion to Christ had begun early in his life when he accepted the call to the priesthood his senior year of high school, making vows of poverty and chastity and the following year making a pilgrimage to Jerusalem. It was there in the holy city that God placed in his heart a fire of insatiable devotion that burgeoned from the Roman Catholic order of Jesuit in the Society of Jesus to priest, bishop and now monsignor. But nothing could have prepared him for this.

"You… you are the Papal," he said. "The first of the Popes and the one in whom the church was founded."

Peter gazed at the floor and put his hands over his face, the monsignor's words igniting a sense of shame. "This is more than I can bear—" Peter confessed. For a moment he gathered his thoughts, not wanting to distress the elder priest, but realizing it had to be addressed. He waited long enough to ensure his words were bathed in love. "You must understand, the church was not to be, nor could it ever be built upon me. I—I am merely a man… an apostle yes, a witness to Christ and His teachings of course, but nothing more than this. Christ alone is the foundation and head of His church."

Peter's words were adamant and unyielding. He hadn't considered that the church had not been established at the point of his ascent through time, yet he had full knowledge of its inception. It was one more in a series of unexplained events he had decided not to explore.

"Jesus called me Petros," he went on. "A small stone as the Greeks would translate it. This language exists still?"

"Yes… well a form of it," Sergetti conceded.

"Then the Scriptures must define my place in what you refer to as Christendom."

"But you were clearly the head of the apostles," Sergetti maintained.

For a moment Peter seemed to look straight through him. "The spokesman if you will. A fellow elder. But do not marvel at this… we were all part of the church's foundation. James, John, Matthew, all of us. We were all little stones, but the mason most assuredly was Christ."

After several dubious moments, a beatific smile crept across the elder priest's face, as if there was understanding beyond his years of training.

"And He is the cornerstone," Sergetti added with certainty.

Peter took the elder priest by the nape of the neck and pulled him to his chest. Sergetti was so emotionally moved that he collapsed into Peter's embrace, hugging him with deference as if he never wanted to let go.

Sixty-Five

April 11, Saturday, A.M.

"Did you have to kill the man?" Mordecai fumed.

"He started asking questions—putting two and two together. I had no choice," said Yousef. Besides, there's a slight chance he may have survived."

"Well that's just perfect. Now we have a witness who can identify you." Mordecai stood in silence, considering the subterfuge.

"He's in critical condition. He'll die."

"You'd better hope so."

"He will. And we both know dead men tell no tales."

"Well, this one might."

Yousef waited the for other shoe to drop.

"We intercepted a text that made it through to the young doctor—Elizabeth Stewart."

"So?"

"So—they know Bernstein was shot."

"They were going to find out eventually."

"But there are surely cameras in the hospital. They know what you look like fool."

"Looks can be deceiving."

"This is a game to you isn't it?"

Yousef's face twisted into a devious grin.

"More coffee sir?"

Paul slid his cup toward the waitress and smiled. She filled it to the brim. Elizabeth and the professor waved her off.

"Do you remember—" Paul stopped long enough to make sure they were out of earshot before continuing. "When we were in the Garden of Gethsemane?"

Elizabeth traded looks with Van Eaton, knowing that he was not with them at the time.

"Jesus said we were the descendants of the Magi."

"The 100th generation as I remember you saying," Van Eaton chimed in, still a bit miffed that he hadn't been there.

Elizabeth smiled, "Yes, I've thought about it a lot this past week."

"We all have I'm sure," Paul went on. "Well do you remember that after they found the child they decided not to go back to Herod?"

They both nodded guardedly.

"Well, I have the strangest feeling that we're not supposed to go back to Mordecai either," he said. "Does that sound crazy?"

Van Eaton stared at Paul for a moment in reflective silence. "No," he confessed. "I've been thinking the same thing."

Elizabeth smiled at the thought. "I think we all have. So what do we need to do from here?"

"We've got to find Peter."

"Of course. You know I'd forgotten that this is his Sabbath," Van Eaton said. "He'd mentioned it on the plane—"

Elizabeth sat up straight, "I wonder if that would have anything to do with where he is?"

"It could," Paul surmised. "I wonder where the nearest

synagogue would be?"

Van Eaton dabbed his mouth with his handkerchief. "He didn't seem overly concerned that it was his Sabbath when we talked about it on the plane," he said.

"I don't know about a synagogue, but I overheard a couple that was in here earlier say that there is an Easter Vigil at St. Patrick's today," Paul said.

Elizabeth smiled. "You know, I can't think of a better place for us to gather our thoughts and pray about all of this—" She searched both men's faces for approval. They were already smiling.

The walk from the coffee shop to St. Patrick's would take about twenty minutes according to the GPS on Elizabeth's phone so they decided to walk. The morning air was brisk, their breath fogging the air as they hurried down the street, stoked with hope that they would soon find Peter.

Sixty-Six

April 11, Saturday, A.M.

"I don't quite know how to say this," the monsignor paused, meeting Peter's gaze. "But how is it that you came to be here in the first place?" he asked, his mind reeling at all of the possibilities.

"Well—" Peter stalled, taking in a deep breath. Then, for the next hour he explained how he came to meet Paul, Elizabeth and the professor in his own time and how he had followed them to the future.

The elder priest could see the physical and emotional drain being separated from his friends had caused, not to mention his apparent lack of sleep. He settled back on the pew, so engrossed in Peter's story that it hadn't occurred to him to question how he was able to understand this Aramaic speaking apostle from a time and place long since passed.

"—After we arrived there at the inn, we decided to walk to the *time square*."

"Times Square?"

"Yes, I believe that was the name. And we came to a grotto he called a sub—sub—"

"Subway?"

"Yes. And now, by a strange turn of events, I find myself here with you," he explained, holding up his hands and wagging his head in disbelief. "How did this happen?"

Sergetti smiled. "I don't know, but somehow I knew it would. I've known for some time. And there is absolutely no doubt that it was God's doing."

Peter sat for a moment in reflective silence, his gaze drifting to the ceiling. He wiped his face, driving sleep from his eyes as he considered the events of the past week and how God had orchestrated those events to bring him here.

"God is the author it is certain. And I wish I could say that my faith has remained strong, but that would be, how do you say—*a lie*." Peter's words carried a hint of remorse.

Sergetti shared a meaningful glance with the apostle. His words carried such an air of innocence and virtue that worries of the drought in his own life quickly faded. And not just in his personal life, but also the burdens he carried for his parish.

"You had mentioned the Waldorf—"

"Yes, yes!" Peter pulled out the card Paul had given him and slid it into Sergetti's hand. "This is where we were to stay for the evening."

Sergetti took the card and pulled out his cell phone. He punched in the numbers.

"Ask for Paul," Peter said.

"What's his last name?"

Peter just looked at Sergetti. "Last name?"

The monsignor thought for a moment, then pressed the END button.

Sixty-Seven

April 11, Saturday, A.M.

Eyes red and temper short, Mordecai paced the floor of his lavish suite, his footfalls silenced by the fibers of a lush, Persian rug. He stopped for a moment and drew back the curtain that spanned the length of the wall. His breath fogged the glass as he looked out over the city. It was vibrant, even at such an early hour. The city that never sleeps rang true to its name.

It had been over an hour since he'd heard anything from his contact, inept as he was. He slid on his readers to assure that his cell phone was charged and the signal was good. Then it trilled.

"They've left the coffee shop and they are headed for St. Patrick's," he said, tugging at his fingerless gloves.

"And how do you know this?"

"When they left, I found a napkin on the table where the woman had been scribbling." He smoothed it out in his palm. "It says *St. Patrick's, 5th Avenue* along with some other scribbling. And it looks like they're headed that way."

Mordecai pulled the phone from his face and put him on speaker. "Listen to me, do not let them out of your sight, do you understand me?" He tried to conceal his irritation, but wasn't entirely successful.

"No sir, I won't."

"And keep me informed! We have got to find Jonah."

"And if they find Jonah there? Is that where you want it done?"

There was a brief silence.

"Yes."

Mordecai pressed the end button and punched in another number. It rang once.

"It appears that they are heading to St. Patrick's Cathedral."

"Appears?"

"That's all we have to go on for now."

"And what of Jonah?"

"Still nothing, but I think they're getting close."

Yousef's jaw tightened. "I will be there within the hour."

Mordecai ended the call. *An hour? I thought he was in Israel?*

Sixty-Eight

April 11, Saturday, A.M.

"You need to get some sleep," Sergetti insisted. "According to what you've told me you've been up for more than twenty-four hours. You've got to be worn out."

The apostle produced a scant smile, but his eyes betrayed him. He knew Sergetti was right, he just didn't want to give in to it—not yet anyway. There were still too many unanswered questions. Too many stones left unturned. Where were his friends? And why had God even allowed him to step on that *sub-way* in the first place? It didn't seem to make any sense. But then again, he knew that logic rarely applied when God was at work—and He was definitely at work. He could sense it deep in his soul as he considered the writings of Isaiah; *'His thoughts are not our thoughts, nor are His ways our ways...'*

"This is my Shabbat," Peter went on. "I should get some rest. But I must admit, we did not always adhere to all of the dictates of the law," he confessed. "In truth, the Master himself did not readily practice many of the ordinances put forth in the law." He smiled at the thought of it.

Sergetti joined him in the thought, still mesmerized by the whole situation. "Tomorrow will be the holiest of our Sabbaths," he began. "And this being Holy Saturday, we will begin our Easter Vigil at eleven this morning and every two hours thereafter until midnight," he explained, not really knowing how much Peter understood about the workings of the church. "The church will be filled to capacity in the next hour or so and it will be that way all day."

"What would you have me to do?" Peter asked. "Can I help you in some way?"

Sergetti took the measure of his tone, knowing all too well that Peter was at the point of total exhaustion. "Come, follow me," he said.

† † †

Sergetti led Peter away from the nave, passing through a series of hallways before coming to a door that looked like a housekeeping closet. He invited Peter to join him inside.

"This is my personal rectory," Sergetti said, turning the key and entering the room. "You'll be safe here and more importantly, undisturbed."

The monsignor flipped on the light, illuminating a windowless room, perhaps twelve feet deep and no more than ten feet across. A single bed stood center of the room. It was wrapped with crisp sheets, military style down to the folds in the blanket tucked neatly between the mattress and springs. A lone wooden crucifix adorned the otherwise barren wall above the headboard and a painting of Da Vinci's Last Supper hung above a narrow wooden desk on the adjacent wall. They were the only decorations in the otherwise modest chambers. On the right was an ordinary chifforobe and a rosary lay coiled atop the center of its chest-of-drawers. A bargain-basement lamp, hardly befitting the monsignor's position, was perched atop the nightstand beside the bed and his Bible lay open beside it. This was home, modest as it was and had been for more years than he cared to remember since he had taken vows of poverty and chastity.

Peter took it all in and smiled. "Thank you, I may be able to sleep indeed."

Sixty-nine

April 11, Saturday, A.M.

"Welcome to St. Patrick's," said the greeter. Her smile was warm and cordial as she handed each of them a program. Inside the stately narthex, the three weary travelers filtered in with the local parishioners and visitors buzzing with small talk, all gathered in expectation of the annual Easter Vigil.

Entering the sanctuary, the time travelers worked their way down the aisle past fluted marble columns, bathed in the light of stained glass portraits that lined the upper mezzanine on both sides. Finally they found a pew with space for the three of them together.

"I'm almost jealous," Paul whispered to Elizabeth, sliding in and sitting down on the cushioned pew.

"I've never been in a Catholic church," she said. "It's so beautiful."

Van Eaton smiled to himself without remark, having been there as a young man with his wife, Carolyn. It had changed little since then. He brushed the thought away.

"Well, here we are," Elizabeth whispered with expectancy. Quietly, she reached for both men's hands as they collectively lifted their petitions for Peter.

† † †

In the stillness of the moment, the majestic *Gallery* pipe organ began a soft recitation of *Be Still My Soul*, setting the mood while the congregation stilled. It was almost as if God was there, wafting through the resonance of every tone and the timbre of every note that was played. And all three sensed it, as if it was something meant solely for them.

In the quiet of the moment, Paul leaned toward Elizabeth. "What was happening?" he asked, giving her the strangest look.

With knitted brows Elizabeth brought her hand to her chest and drew in a stuttering breath. She tried to speak but couldn't, nor could Van Eaton, who sat in silence.

If God had gone silent, He was certainly making up for it now, Paul thought. *This is exactly where we're supposed to be, there is no doubt.*

† † †

Some rows back, a stealthy figure slipped between two pews and sat down. He removed his fingerless gloves, put them on his lap and adjusted the shoulder holster under his jacket.

SEVENTY

April 11, Saturday, A.M.

The monsignor climbed the six steps to the lectern platform. He picked up his lavalier microphone and secured it to his vestment. For a moment, he gazed out over the crowd. *These congregants have no idea how meaningful this service will be,* he thought. He made the Sign of the Cross and began.

"We believe in one God—" they all began in chorus. "The Father almighty, maker of heaven and earth, of all things visible and invisible. And in one Lord Jesus Christ, the only Son of God, begotten from the Father before all ages, God from God, Light from Light, true God from true God, begotten, not made…"

The monsignor drew a slight breath as he continued the rote recitation. He'd delivered it more times than he could remember over his forty-plus years since joining the Jesuit order. Now, the Nicene Creed as it had come to be known, had taken on a new significance since his encounter with Peter. As he spoke and looked out over the congregation, for a fleeting moment, he contemplated sharing his situation. *Has my brain gone numb?* he wondered. *The Apostle Peter himself, literally the first Pope of the Roman Catholic*

Church is here within the walls of St. Patrick's and not a soul is privy to it. His pulse raced at the very thought of revealing it and yet, in his spirit he knew it was not the thing to do. He knew full well that God had chosen him to be a part of something that was bigger than him—bigger than anything he could imagine. And he had no intentions of jeopardizing such a mission.

He bowed with modest reverence and kissed the scriptures.

"My dear friends. We welcome you to St. Patrick's by reciting the blessed Nicene Creed, a statement of faith that expresses the devotion that each of the apostles had to Jesus's life, death and resurrection. It also promises such a resurrection to us all. What an amazing and glorious gift!" His words echoed through the enormous cathedral, spreading through the congregation like seeds on fertile ground.

"All of this is ours because God offered us His Son to come to his earthly kingdom to live, to teach, to perform miracles and yet to suffer and to die for our sins as Jesus of Nazareth. We know this through the stories told to us by the apostles, who witnessed the miracles, the joys, the suffering and the glory of Jesus's rebirth. Imagine the apostles' pain in seeing their leader, their spiritual guide, crucified. Yet they had been told that He would rise from the dead on the third day, Easter Sunday."

Sergetti moved to the side of the lectern and steadied himself, a shroud of calm enveloping him.

"That day, Mary Magdalene was the first to see Jesus risen from the dead. Several others saw him, and then, to his great joy, Peter became the first apostle to see Jesus alive. Just imagine how he felt as Jesus told Peter that he would be the rock upon which Jesus would build His church—and it makes me wonder, what would we say to Peter if he was here today?"

Paul's eyes darted from Elizabeth to Van Eaton and back as they all considered the irony.

"I believe I would thank him for his bravery in watching our Savior suffer. For his humility and devotion to being the leader of apostles. And I would thank him for his willingness to build the church to which Jesus was, and is, the cornerstone."

Sergetti paused and looked out over the congregation, wanting desperately to continue, but knowing full well he could not.

He moved back behind the lectern and closed his Bible.

"Now if you will, please bow your heads and join with me. Our Father, who art in heaven, hallowed be thy name, thy kingdom come, thy will be done on earth as it is in heaven—"

After a beat the congregation stirred and moved into the aisles as the monsignor stepped down from the podium and walked toward the rear chambers set aside for clergy. Paul shouldered his way to the front as he watched the priest handshake his way through the crowd until he was able to touch the priest on the sleeve.

"Father—" The salutation felt strange to him.

Sergetti turned and made eye contact, his thoughts dissolving into a tentative smile. "Yes my son, how may I help you?"

"I wonder if we might speak somewhere in private?"

The monsignor led them to the sacristy. He placed his vestments on the valet and smoothed them as the three entered the room.

"Please, have a seat," he said, motioning them to two pews.

"Thank you." Paul licked his lips and smiled, visibly stalling.

"Ah, father, my name is Paul Ryann and this is Dr. Elizabeth Stewart and Professor Van Eaton."

"Leonardo," Van Eaton insisted.

Sergetti smiled and nodded gently as if he knew more than he was letting on, simply because he did. In fact he was screaming on the inside. Of course he knew who they were from his conversation with Peter. But he wanted to keep that knowledge to himself… for the time being anyway.

"I am Monsignor Joseph Sergetti," he said with a modest tenor. "And how may I be of service to you?"

Paul collected his thoughts and glanced at Elizabeth as if seeking consent.

"Thank you for taking the time to meet with us. I too am a pastor," Paul offered. "I guess having someone drop in unannounced after a service is one of the perks, huh?" he said with a hint of sarcasm. Ordinarily that provoked a laugh, but not this time. *So much for the small talk—*

Sergetti only grinned.

"Before we go any further, could we pray for just a moment?" Paul asked with a sense of urgency in his voice.

The four immediately postured themselves and bowed their heads, but nothing could have prepared them for what was about to happen.

"Father—" Paul began. "We come to you with open hearts and minds as we seek your guidance. Help us to follow as you lead us in the way we should go, not trusting in our own abilities, but in yours. And help us to know that we are in your perfect will as we—as we share with our brother the things we are about to share. We pray this in Jesus' most precious name, amen."

Before they could open their eyes, the doorknob turned and a man barged inside, his finger curled around the trigger of a Glock 19.

SEVENTY-ONE
April 11, Saturday, A.M.

Liz drew a sharp intake of breath, looking first at the man with the gun, and then at Paul. Her startled eyes said everything.

"If you want to live you'll stay right where you are—" the man ordered. "And keep your hands where I can see them." He shook frantically as he pointed the Glock at each of their heads. With the other hand he thumbed numbers on his phone.

"It's me—" There was a long pause. "No, he's not with them but—" He gave a side-eye and his jaw tightened. "No sir, but I plan to—" Another pause. "Yes sir, I understand." He pressed the end button and seethed. He walked to the center of the room and stopped.

"Where is he?"

Elizabeth exchanged glances with Paul and the professor. "Who?"

"You know who I'm talking about! Jonah!"

"Why are you doing this?" Elizabeth scolded.

"Shut up!" he shouted, scratching his temple with the gun barrel. "I have to think!"

Like a caged animal, the would-be assassin began pacing back and forth across the room. As he turned and started away from them, Sergetti eased out of his chair and toward a side door. To cover his escape, the professor suddenly slammed his hand down hard on the heavy wooden pew where he was sitting, simultaneously screaming. "This is insane!"

A split second later, Liz and Paul watched in horror as a bullet smashed through the professor's cheek and his body immediately went limp and tumbled to the floor. Liz spun around and buried her head in Paul's chest.

In the melee, the man quickly abandoned his hellish mission, disappearing as soon as the bullet left the gun. Head down, he slipped the weapon back into the holster and pushed through the crowd until he was far enough to blend in. He slowed his pace to keep from bringing attention to himself until he made it outside and ultimately disappeared.

Elizabeth was immobilized by shock… visions of Afghanistan flashed through her brain as she struggled to gain control of the situation. "We've got to get out of here!" Paul said. Without skipping a beat he hooked his arm around her waist and dragged her toward the door. Liz composed herself enough to get free and check for a pulse on Van Eaton, even though it was more than apparent he was gone. His face was a bloody mask, his eyes fixed and dilated.

† † †

Sergetti worked his way down the back side of the sacristy and toward his room. And even though he heard the gunshot, there was no way he was going back. His mind was solely on Peter. Fumbling with the key, he turned the dead bolt and darted into the room.

"Wake up! Come! Get up!"

Sergetti's pleas were convincing enough, but Peter was still a little slow in waking and remembering where he was. He smeared the sleep from his eyes and sat up. "What is it?!"

"We must hurry Peter! There are bad people looking for you!"

"But where—why?"

"Please trust me, we have to go," Sergetti insisted. He helped Peter to his feet.

As Peter buttoned his shirt, he noticed the bullet hole, but made no comment.

"There are catacombs beneath this very church," Sergetti said. "I'm going to take you there."

Seventy-two

April 11, Saturday, A.M.

Sergetti took Peter by the arm and led him down the hallway toward the access to the catacombs. Ahead, a narrow passageway led to a stone stairway that circled several times before descending into the darkness. Peter, now completely winded, stopped at the top of the staircase to catch his breath. He pulled out the photo he had torn from the magazine on the plane. Unfolding the image, he handed it to Sergetti.

"This is Times Square no?" he asked between deep breaths.

"Yes," Sergetti said. He too was winded, but not as much as Peter.

"This is where I am to go," Peter insisted.

Sergetti studied the picture, his eyes glazing over as he mulled the thought. "I think I know what we're supposed to do," he said. "Are you up for a journey on foot?"

Peter sucked in a breath and let it out. "I think so."

Sergetti took Peter by the arm and led him down the staircase and into the darkness.

† † †

Paul opened the sacristy door just enough to get a glimpse of what was going on outside. Chaos.

He eased the door shut and pressed his forehead against it. "There are people everywhere," he said. His pulse raced.

He turned and watched Elizabeth take Sergetti's vestment from the valet and drape it over Van Eaton's body. She looked at Paul with tear-filled eyes. "He deserves better than this."

"Yes he does—but we need to get out of here now!" Paul said. The words hung in the air as their thoughts merged. They both spied the door that only moments ago Sergetti used to escape. A minute later they filtered into the crowd unnoticed. And though there was no one there that looked official, they both decided that it was best for them not to get involved with police asking questions they didn't want to answer.

Seventy-Three

April 11, Saturday, A.M.

Two majestic, hand-hewn cypress doors stood in the arched entrance of the shadowy catacombs. Sergetti went to the wall and punched the numbers on the security system—then he loosened the slide bar and heaved open the doors. The room was magnificent. The entryway was easily ten-feet thick and laden with hand-chiseled stonework that formed the arch from floor to ceiling. Inside, the vaults themselves lined the passageway on both sides. Each was individually lighted and bore the names of the charter parishioners and the families of those who founded the cathedral. But there was little time to take notice as Peter and the monsignor hurried through the corridor.

At the end, a patchwork of smooth marble stones formed a solid wall that spanned the width of the corridor maybe twenty feet across. The stones themselves were not mortared and there were no uneven seams. Sergetti placed his left hand in the center of one particular stone and put his right hand on another. With all his might he pushed and a section of the wall pivoted and an opening appeared.

"I discovered this door several years ago, but I never said

anything to anyone about it. For the life of me I didn't know why… until now."

"God had a plan," Peter said matter-of-factly. The two of them pushed the wall open enough to get through. Once inside, they heaved the door back into place with a thud and the darkness engulfed them. In the pitch blackness Sergetti retrieved his cellphone and punched in the flashlight app, illuminating the room. But there was no visible re-entry point. There was not even a seam.

"We're committed now," he said with a grave tone. He turned and inspected the room that was actually a large tunnel, tall enough for a person to stand, with a flat floor that was at best, two feet across. Both the walls and floor had been meticulously formed with blue gneiss stones that were part of the primary foundation material when the church was built. Unfortunately, he'd not ventured far past the door when he first discovered it but now he wished he had.

"This appears to be a limb off of a main artery of storm sewers that serve the city," he explained to Peter, illuminating both of their faces. "For whatever reason, after I discovered this place, I spent hours in the library researching the underground maze that serves the city. And I discovered something I haven't even thought about in years until you showed me that picture. This is part of the Gateway project that connects New York with New Jersey. And I know for a fact this tunnel ultimately leads to Times Square!"

† † †

It was a good mile trek back to the hotel, but Liz and Paul both thought it would be a good time to clear their heads. Liz wept gently and her shoulders bobbed as they walked while Paul stayed on high alert watching for basically anything or anyone that looked suspicious.

The trauma of seeing the professor killed was horrifying both in its violence and in the personal tragedy of losing their friend—a man who had shared with them an experience no other person on

Earth would ever truly understand. That kind of heaviness wasn't easy to carry.

"What do you think happened to the priest?"

Paul looked at Liz with mixed emotions. "I don't know, but more than likely he's already talking to the police which means they'll have our physical descriptions."

"This is crazy," Liz said. "We just went there to try and find Peter, and now Van Eaton—"

Paul looked up. "Hey, there's a deli across the street. Let's duck in there and sit for a few minutes."

Inside, they found a table in the back where no one could see them from the street. Within a minute, a waiter with a notepad and a pencil at-the-ready came over.

"What'll you have?"

Paul glanced at the menu. "Two coffees and two bagels with cream cheese, please."

"Got it." He walked away barking at the cook, "Two burned and split with cheese and two black eyes."

Both Liz and Paul tried to smile at the waiter's orders, but it was short lived. "Do you have any idea what's going on? Why is the professor dead? Our cantankerous professor turned hero." She began to weep again.

"I don't have the faintest idea what's going on. One morning I got up and brushed my teeth and the next thing I know I'm starring in one million years BC."

Liz just looked at Paul.

"I'm sorry. This isn't funny. Sometimes when I don't know how to handle a serious situation I resort to inappropriate humor."

"It's all right. We're all under enormous pressure. I'd venture to say there are few people in the world who have ever experienced such pressure. So, why us?"

Paul pulled a napkin from the holder and wiped his mouth. "Well, it's clear that we've traveled through time as a result of God's plan, that much I'm certain of. But I think there are other forces at play here."

"What do you mean?"

Paul glanced around the room and lowered his voice.

"I mean evil forces Liz. Who was that curator—Yousef who shot Bernstein? And what about Mordecai? I hate to say it, but you were right on the plane when you said you were having doubts about him. I should have listened to you."

Elizabeth formed a tight lipped smile. *No sense in beating him up over it,* she thought.

"You know, the Bible describes the ongoing battle between good and evil, and this is one heck of an example of how far Satan will go to try to steer souls away from their Heavenly home."

The trill of Liz's phone unexpectedly intruded.

"Oh, no, who could this be? I don't recognize the number."

She handed Paul her phone.

"Hello, Elizabeth Stewart's phone, this is Paul Ryann."

"How do you do, Paul. This is your wife."

"Darling, how are you? I'm sorry my phone was turned off. I've been waiting till we got back to the hotel to call you. Is everything okay?" He made an "uh-oh" face at Liz who could tell by the tenor of the woman's voice that Paul and his wife weren't having an especially warm conversation.

"Honey, it's just been a hectic day. Can I call you in about an hour?"

"Yes, honey, I'm safe." He made another face. "You know I love you. I'll call you in a little bit."

Paul pushed the end button and handed the phone back to Liz. "I forgot to tell you I had given her your number. I'm sorry."

"That's perfectly fine Paul, I'm just sorry I didn't answer it to give you time to compose yourself. I hope she doesn't think ill of me."

"On the contrary, I told her all about you and the professor before we left Israel. She seemed fine with everything."

Elizabeth smiled and shook her head. "I pray to God that I find a husband who loves me like you love Laura."

Paul returned the smile.

The waiter arrived balancing their plates on one arm and holding two cups of coffee in the other. He placed the check on the table as two squad cars whizzed past.

"We need to go." He placed two tens on the table and left the food. "We need to get to the hotel and get our things."

SEVENTY-FOUR

April 11, Saturday, P.M.

Sludge-coated electrical and plumbing conduits lined the sewer walls, connecting them to a network of passageways under the city. As they ventured farther, Sergetti's sense of direction was now completely lost. To add to the ambiance, rats crept along pipes on both sides of the tunnel and it almost seemed as if the rodents were following them. Peter stopped long enough to clear a stone from his sandal and when he reached to steady himself, he squashed a cockroach with a crunch.

"This is not the most pleasant of places," he admitted, wiping the remnants of the roach on his pants.

"It shouldn't be much further," Sergetti said, not so confidently.

As they walked, vertical shafts spaced every 100 feet or so shot straight up to the street above, and an iron ladder was affixed to each shaft. At the top of every one, a manhole cover was perched and beams of sunlight flashed intermittently as cars rolled over them, rattling the iron covers like hammers striking an anvil. At least that's how Peter perceived it.

Sergetti, on the other hand, had hardly noticed the goings-on above. He was more concerned with how they were going to make it out of there and when they did, what would their next step be? His thoughts ran in circles.

† † †

The phone rang twice before Mordecai picked it up. He looked at the face and pressed the *accept* button.

"Well?" He waited.

"I ah, I had a situation and well, I wanted you to hear it from me before you heard it from someone else."

"I'm listening."

"I had to kill the professor."

"You did what?" He combed his fingers through his oily gray hair and slammed his fist on the bedside table.

"I had no choice, he tried to rush me." He knew he was lying, but he wasn't about to take the fall if he could weasel his way out of it.

"You killed the professor? Have you lost your mind?" Mordecai pulled the phone from his ear and covered the mouthpiece. *I will kill him with my bare hands,* he said to himself. When he returned the henchman was still talking.

"—And he was collateral damage."

"Collateral damage? You don't even know the meaning of the word!" There were more ramblings. "Shut up you fool! I want Jonah, do you understand me? I want Jonah! And I don't care what it takes do you understand? Even if you have to kill the other two. I want Jonah! Have I made myself clear?"

"I understand."

"Do you?"

"Yes sir, but—the church has got to be crawling with cops by now."

"That's your problem, just get back over there and find them and don't let them out of your sight until you hear from me!"

"Yes sir."

† † †

The hotel is right around the corner," Paul said. "I'm hoping we can make it to the elevator without being seen."

He reached the revolving doors first and Elizabeth slid in the compartment behind him. As they followed the door around, Paul caught sight of Mordecai standing in the lobby. He hid his face and walked the revolving door around until it opened again outside. Elizabeth followed.

"Did you see Mordecai?"

"Yes! And did you see who he was talking to?"

Paul wagged his head.

"I think it was Yousef!"

"No, are you sure?"

"I think so… but how? How could he be here? He was in Israel when we were. How did he—"

The hair on the back of Paul's neck bristled. "It's all beginning to make sense now," he said.

"What do you mean?"

"Never mind. Maybe we can find another way in."

SEVENTY-FIVE

April 11, Saturday, P.M.

Sergetti looked up through the dark shaft that led to the street above. His breath fogged the air. "The best I can tell we're either very close to Times Square or twice as far away as when we started. If I could get close enough to the top, I might be able to pick up a signal on my GPS."

Peter watched with the most trusting eyes as Sergetti ascended the ladder and made his way toward the top of the shaft. The rusted, metal rungs of the ladder were ice cold and coated with, whatever it was, he didn't want to know. When he reached the top, he held the phone up in search of a signal. Nothing. Not one bar. And to add to the disparity, his battery was down to 5%. He cautiously descended back down the ladder and dropped into the ankle deep water.

"The cover… it cannot be removed? Peter asked.

"No it's not that. I was able to pick up enough of a signal to tell that we went the wrong way." Sergetti shook his head in disgust. "We're twice as far from Times Square as when we started."

"Perhaps we should climb out through one of the covers."

"Most of them are in the middle of the street—" Sergetti

explained. "And I read that they've either been locked or welded shut since 911…"

911. For a moment Peter considered the significance of the numerals.

"We need to pray for God's guidance," Sergetti went on.

Peter smiled and slipped his arm around Sergetti. "From the moment we entered the tunnel."

† † †

There was no one at the side entrance when Paul slid his keycard through the slot. It worked. And since his and Elizabeth's rooms were both on the second floor they decided to use the stairs.

Paul flipped on the light and immediately closed the drapes, not taking any chances on someone spotting them from outside. "We've got to be careful," he said with a sense of urgency.

Liz took the measure of his tone. "What did you mean when you said it was all beginning to make sense?"

Paul contemplated the question. "I'm going to say something here that you might think is crazy, but just hear me out."

Elizabeth waited.

"I always thought there was something strange about Yousef," he admitted. "From that first day we met him at the Garden Tomb I had a check in my spirit. And I don't wanna scare you, but—"

"What?"

He walked to the window and turned. "I don't know how to say this but, I don't think he's who he says he is. In fact, I don't think he's human at all." He waited, not knowing how Elizabeth would take him. When he again made eye contact, she was still processing.

"You know, I think Satan would do anything to keep Peter from accomplishing what he has come here to do," Liz surmised.

"I agree, but it would be nice to know what that was."

"Yes it would."

"In the meantime we just have to keep vigilant… and we've

got to find Peter."

"Absolutely. Above all else."

† † †

Twenty minutes had passed when there was a sharp knock at the door.

Liz glanced at Paul and went to the door. "Yes?"

"Room service."

Paul shushed her away and opened the door a crack to check out the voice. He stepped back and let the room service attendant make his delivery. The server quickly set up service for two at the table and handed Paul the check to initial.

Paul sat down, not waiting for Liz to join him. When she finally sat down, he apologized as he chewed his first bite of steak. It was tough but good. "I didn't realize how much energy I had expended until I smelled the food."

Liz watched in amazement as Paul scarfed down his food. She draped a napkin across her lap and said a quick prayer. Her chef salad looked meager by comparison, but she knew she had to eat at least some of it. She couldn't remember the last time she had eaten and she knew she had to keep her strength up, but all she could feel was empathy; she was also feeling drained, but it was more from stress than exertion.

"I really don't feel like eating—" she said, her voice trailing. "But I know I need to. It's just—I can still see his face." She looked at Paul, her eyes welling with tears. "But this isn't like me. I've seen this kind of thing before. Afghanistan… even my regular job as an air-evac nurse. But somehow this is different," she said in a soft, but valid voice.

"I know." Paul put his fork down and propped his elbows on the table, threading his fingers together. "I feel the same way, I'm just trying not to think about it. Another one of my defense mechanisms."

"I understand," she said. "But I'm afraid we're going to have to think about getting out of here. When they find out the professor's identity it will just be a matter of time before they link us to all of this."

Paul thought for a moment. "You know what? I need to call my bride. Would you give me a minute?"

Elizabeth pulled out her key card. "I'll be in my room next door freshening up."

† † †

"Hey honey, is this a good time?

"Yes of course."

"Good. I just wanted to call you and tell you that I love you. And that I'm sorry I've been so preoccupied."

Laura seemed relieved that Paul had called her back so quickly. "I understand, I was just concerned that you were cutting your trip short that's all. This trip meant so much to you."

"You have no idea… it was the trip of a lifetime."

"But you were only gone a few days, how—"

"I'll be able to explain everything to you when I get home," he said.

"And when do you think that will be?"

"Soon hopefully. We had to divert here to New York last night because of the weather, but we hope to be on our way home soon."

"That reminds me, I got a call earlier from someone who said they were with Mount Olive Medical."

"Who was it?"

"They didn't say, but I didn't tell them anything. I just said they'd have to call back."

A chill snaked up Paul's spine. He wanted to tell Laura everything, but he just couldn't bring himself to do so. Not yet. "Well, let me know if they call back."

"I will."

"You're my soulmate you know," Paul said, fighting back tears.

"You're mine," she replied.

He pressed the end button and grabbed his jacket. He went next door and knocked on Elizabeth's door.

"We've got to get out of here now," he said.

Liz slid on her coat. "I think I've got an idea—"

SEVENTY-SIX

April 11, Saturday, P.M.

Paul followed Elizabeth down the stairs and out the side entrance.

On the street, a police car whizzed past, lights and sirens blaring, then another. Paul was careful to cover his face as they passed, not knowing if they were heading to St. Patrick's or on another call, but either way he couldn't take a chance.

"Just walk normal," he said.

Elizabeth chewed on a cuticle and walked to the corner. She bought a scarf from a street vendor and wound it loosely around her neck. Then she pulled a ball cap from a rack and gave it to Paul. She gave the man a twenty.

Paul pulled the cap down hard against his head and looked at Elizabeth. She was already out with her phone, thumb-typing "Times Square" on her *Uber app*. She showed it to Paul.

"That's a good idea. What better place to hide than in a crowd."

"I'm showing three Ubers tracking this way," she said.

Paul nodded.

Two police cars in full chase mode passed over the manhole cover, disregarding the red light as they weaved in and out of traffic, the sound fading with them as they passed. Thirty feet below, Peter and Sergetti heard the sirens, but paid little attention.

"I wonder what happened to them?" Peter heard Sergetti mumble to himself.

"What?"

"Before I came to get you, I had just sat down to a meeting with some people that came to me after the service…" Sergetti explained.

Peter stopped and straddled the water as he listened.

Sergetti moved closer to Peter who could now see tears glistening in his eyes. "It was your friends," Sergetti admitted. "Paul, Elizabeth and the professor."

Peter unwittingly shook his head. "But why did you not tell me?" He watched Sergetti's face in the faint light.

"Because, I'm afraid something has happened to one of them… maybe all of them." He turned away and collected his thoughts. "A man came in with a gun. Do you know what—"

"I know what a gun is, to my misfortune," Peter said, rubbing his stomach.

"Well, when I saw a chance to escape I knew I had to get to you," Sergetti explained. "Then when I was in the hallway I heard a gunshot, but I knew there was nothing I could do." Sergetti smeared the tears from his face. "I am so ashamed. I should have gone back."

Peter embraced Sergetti and held him there. "You did what you thought was best to protect me," he said. "You risked your life for me. No greater love has any man than this."

Seventy-Seven

April 11, Saturday, P.M.

"We got a name?" Detective Don Thetford seemed almost too casual as he slid a pair of throw-a-ways over his black brogues and ducked under the police tape. The sight was heinous. A pool of coagulating blood surrounded Van Eaton's torso and brain matter seemed to be everywhere, even in places where you wouldn't think it should be. But he remained focused, carefully kneeling beside the body.

"Do we know who put this robe over the body?"

"No sir, when we got here it was already like this," said the adjutant.

"Any witnesses?"

"Nobody has come forward yet, but this man said he saw three people go in with the monsignor—two men and a woman, right after the service." Thetford looked up at a fiftyish Hispanic man dressed in industrial greens. "—Says he's the custodian."

"Put him with an artist and maybe we'll get lucky—does he speak English?"

"Si, a little," he answered.

With a pen, Thetford peeled back the vestment and looked into the blood splattered face of Professor Van Eaton. "Was this one of the people you saw come in here?"

The custodian gasped and shook noticeably. "Ya—yes."

"Take him outside," the detective ordered. And close that door!"

Thetford cinched his latex gloves up at his wrists. "No rigor yet, but it won't be long," he said. He glanced at his watch: 12:55. He gently ran his gloved hand along Van Eaton's breast pocket and removed his wallet.

"Leonardo Van Eaton, lives in Fairfax, VA. Professor at Georgetown. And here's a passport," he mumbled to himself. He opened it and studied the stamps. "Ben Gurion International, Israel just yesterday. New Delhi the day before, and here's another one from Ben Gurion." The only other item was a card he found in Van Eaton's pocket. "The Waldorf Astoria," he read. He turned and handed the passport and wallet to his adjutant, but kept the card. "See that Montrose gets these."

The detective stood with effort. "What about the monsignor?"

"We haven't been able to locate him."

"So we've got a vic and three missing witnesses, is that right?"

"At this point, yes sir."

"And what's this?" Thetford noticed something pinned under Van Eaton's shoulder. He pulled the body on its side and with his pen, fished out a fingerless glove. He held it up to the light. "Get this to Montrose and have him run a DNA genotype," he said. "And I need it yesterday!"

"Times Square is only about a mile, but everything is backed up right now," the Uber driver said. His middle eastern accent was hardly noticeable, but it was obvious from his name on his license. "Did you hear about the shooting at St. Patrick's?"

Paul glanced at Liz and pulled the door shut. "When?"

"About an hour ago I guess… probably a gang thing," he surmised. "The cops are all over the place."

Liz nudged Paul and he read her lips. *Ask him what happened?*

"Did you hear what happened?"

"Just that somebody got shot—that's all I know. Either way I bet the police will be out everywhere tonight."

Paul looked at Liz as she stared out the window. She was blinking back tears.

Seventy-Eight

April 11, Saturday, P.M.

Mordecai paced a small circle behind the sumptuous live greenery in the Waldorf lobby where he concealed himself as he waited for the police to leave. He cringed when he saw Yousef walk directly in front of the police detectives, craning his neck and looking for Mordecai. He should have known his boss would be out of sight. Mordecai drew out his phone and tapped in Yousef's number.

"Would you please stop looking like a stalker and just follow the carpet to the last huge greenery on your left?"

Yousef stopped just past the entourage of police, and turned slightly to see them, looking suspiciously like a criminal. Mordecai rolled his eyes and shook his head. Meanwhile, Detective Thetford thanked the hotel concierge, leaving a business card and promising to return swiftly should anyone attempt to visit Professor Van Eaton's room.

Seeing the coast was clear, Mordecai showed himself to Yousef, and he walked quickly to his boss.

"We've got a lot of work to do," Mordecai told him.

"I'm always here to assist you," said Yousef.

"So, the two people you met in Israel—the reverend Paul Ryann and the young physician, Elizabeth Stewart are alone now. Our challenge is to find them and get them to lead us to Jonah."

"What about the priest? He was with them at the cathedral."

"Yes, so what's our logical conclusion? Mordecai asked.

"He's with Jonah?"

"Brilliant!" said Mordecai, that one word dripping with sarcasm. "So get on it. We need locations on both groups. Before they figure out a way to reunite."

Well beneath the streets of New York City, another city exists. A vast network of hundreds of miles of tunnels, sewers and subways, built section by section over the last 150 years, connecting areas as far south as Brooklyn to The Bronx on the north side, and Queens on the east side to the banks of the Hudson on the west. During Prohibition it was a haven for speakeasys and myriad illegal escapades. These joints were a hidden labyrinth of illegitimate goings-on that lasted more than two decades in the first half of the twentieth century. Now, this same network had become a lifeline for Sergetti and the apostle.

Ahead, a tunnel they had followed more than a mile came to a confluence of multiple tunnels, creating a vast open space. Sergetti waited for Peter to catch up before stepping down through the opening.

"We're close," he said, his words echoing off the walls.

Sergetti helped Peter down from the opening to the floor. Like everything else, it was wet, but not so much so that it was slick. The air was also cooler and there was a slight breeze.

Then, through the pale darkness there was a rustling sound. Sergetti noticed it first and he turned to Peter, who brought an index finger to his pursed lips.

On the far side of the open space a gauzy figure appeared. As they watched from the shadows, one figure after another made its way through the opening across the room and to the floor below. There was little talking among them, but enough that Sergetti and Peter could sense they were not dangerous. As the last person stepped down, the group gathered in the center of the room and kindled a glowing fire. And as the room became awash in the flickering light, there was no place for Peter or Sergetti to hide. Cautiously the two men came into the light.

Seventy-nine

April 11, Saturday, P.M.

"I know a shortcut if you don't mind a few bumps," the Uber driver said. "They're working on the street, but it's passable—I used it earlier."

"That's fine," Paul said.

As he wheeled through the traffic, the driver dialed something into his phone and glanced in the mirror. Paul was looking right at him. The man quickly diverted his eyes to the road.

Paul nudged Liz and motioned toward the driver but didn't say anything.

"So what's going on at Times Square?" the driver asked in an overly casual tone.

"Sightseeing," they said in unison.

"Not from here?"

"No, we're both from Memphis."

"Ah Elvis Presley." He watched them in the mirror and they both grinned.

Finally they pulled up to a traffic light and stopped. "I think we're going to get out and walk from here," Paul said.

"But we're not to Times Square yet."

"It's ok we need to walk."

The driver shrugged and unlocked the doors.

"Thank you for the lift," Elizabeth said, stepping out. "Your five stars is on the way."

The driver nodded as he drove away.

"Did you see him texting someone while he was driving?" Paul asked.

"No."

"Well, he was… and I'm paranoid."

"Is that why we got out?"

Paul's gaze fell to the street. "Yeah, I'm sorry."

Elizabeth took his hand and painted on a smile. "Times Square is just a few blocks up that way."

EiGHTY

April 11, Saturday, P.M.

"Ahem—" Sergetti tried to tamp down the anxiety he felt. He cleared his throat again, anticipating a reaction from the group, but to his surprise no one moved. He glanced at Peter and shrugged.

The fire provided enough light for them to make out the entire group. Sergetti counted eight or nine apparently homeless people, perched on tire rims and other various refuse. One of them finally spoke.

"Well, what have we here?" said one man in the group. "It's a white collar."

"Yeah well," said an old woman. "What are you doin' down here?" Her raspy voice hinted at a lifetime of abuse.

"That's that preacher from St. Patrick's," another piped up: He brought us food one night when we were on the church steps, you remember *Simon*?" He nudged his friend.

Peter flinched at the sound of his birth name. It was a name he hadn't answered to in years—not since the Master changed it the day they met. He shrugged the thought away.

Sergetti found a small ledge to rest on. Peter looked askance at the not-so-desirable seating, but he needed to get off of his feet. He wondered if Sergetti had a plan.

Then in the distance, there was a scream. And another even louder. There seemed to be little concern among the group, but Peter and Sergetti couldn't help but take notice. And though confused by the sounds ricocheting off the walls, they were able to determine where it was coming from.

"That way," said Peter, pointing through the shadows to one particular opening.

As they began the cautious but deliberate jaunt through the darkness, Peter prayed it wouldn't be another situation like the one he'd faced on the subway. Nevertheless, he knew he was God's servant and part of his calling was to protect the innocent. Given how Sergetti had jumped in to save his life, he was certain he felt the same way.

Without considering rats or roaches or unmentionable debris, the two hurried through the darkness with caution, given that Peter was wearing sandals and that the surface was slick. As they rounded a corner, they came to a sort of tent fashioned by two people holding up the ends of a blanket. There were also others there attending to a young girl in labor, lying on a pile of dingy clothes. The girl, no more than 11 or 12 years old, was sobbing as tears and sweat streaked her face.

"Mama, it's almost here! What do I do now?" the girl begged for directions. Sergetti and Peter looked through faint light at each other, not knowing if they should interrupt, considering neither of them had ever delivered a baby either. But Sergetti had been in plenty of emergency situations and decided he had a certain amount of credit if for no other reason than his age. It was undoubtedly more qualification than that of the young girl.

Sergetti stepped into the light, announcing himself as he prepared to help.

The girl continued to scream. As Sergetti took the corner of the blanket and held it over her, Peter tapped him on the shoulder, indicating they should switch places.

"Where I come from, women frequently give birth in unusual places," Peter said. "I have learned from watching it many times. Maybe you could see if you can find a way out of here—to get some help."

At that, a wormy little man with a toothless smile took Sergetti's hand. "I can show you the way out," he said. Sergetti couldn't have been more relieved. Delivering babies was certainly not in the catechism handbook, although he would have been ready to do so.

At that point, several observers began to walk away as Sergetti interrupted their departure. "Does anyone know how to contact a supervisor or someone who works in the tunnels?"

One person pointed up at a camera mounted high on the wall. "Wave a sign. If they're watching, sometimes they respond," she shrugged. And that was the extent of the advice.

EiGHtY-OnE

April 11, Saturday, P.M.

Every step closer to Times Square brought a strange awareness that Paul and Elizabeth physically sensed. It was as if they knew they were supposed to be there and they welcomed the confirmation of certainty.

"Peter is close," Paul said without preamble. "I can feel it."

A shiver ran down Elizabeth's spine. She too believed it, and it was nice to share the belief with someone she trusted. They crossed at the light and strode up the street like they knew exactly where they were going… as if spiritual intuition guided them.

"It's up the street that way," Liz pointed ahead, trying not to break into an out-and-out run. Paul fell in behind her, winded.

Finally he had to stop. Pausing to take deep breaths, he looked up, not believing his eyes. Elizabeth followed his gaze. "You've got to be kidding me," she said. "Really?"

There it was, in big red letters for the whole world to see. A new hit Broadway musical for the ages… *THE BIG FISHERMAN!*

The monsignor smoothed his hair and straightened his collar as he composed himself and stepped out of the dark tunnel into the light. He stopped briefly to feel the warm afternoon sun on his face. *No time to waste,* he thought. He had to find someone to help; never mind that the authorities were undoubtedly on the lookout for him. But he didn't care, he was on a mission.

At the end of the street, he spied a police officer standing on the corner. He ran without hesitation to him.

"Officer! I need your help!"

"What can I do for ya, fatha?"

"We have a situation—a woman is about to give birth down in the tunnels! I need you to come with me!"

The officer grabbed the mic button on his epaulet alerting Bellevue hospital, requesting an ambulance at Broadway and seventh, stat.

Sergetti ducked through the graffiti-decorated door off the street as the officer followed and they both made their way down a cinderblock hallway. At the end of it, a set of rusted double doors marked the entrance into the tunnels. Sergetti had already propped open one of the doors on his way out, so he grabbed it and flung it open. "This way!" he said.

The two men followed the long set of descending stairs that emptied into a spiderwebbed corridor at the bottom. Flashlight in hand, the officer illuminated their path as he followed Sergetti's lead. They could both hear the woman's screams.

As they approached the site, the screams faded and the cries of a newborn baby took their place. And standing in the midst with a huge grin, Peter was holding a tiny, wrinkled baby boy.

"He looks like a little Methuselah," Sergetti said, obviously winded.

"Oh no," said Peter. "He is a beautiful little child of God."

Eighty-two

April 11, Saturday, P.M.

The EMT propped his leg on the ambulance bumper, balancing an iPad on his knee as he filled out the usual forms. "That was the most amazing thing I've ever seen," he said. "That girl would have died had you not been there to stop the bleeding."

Peter offered a slight nod. "I am glad I was there to assist," he said, absently tracing the large 911 that was printed on the ambulance with his finger.

"Well you certainly did, and I think she wants to say something to you before we take her and the baby to Bellevue—if that's okay." He opened the door and gestured into the ambulance. "Watch your step."

Sergetti remained on the sidewalk trying to keep a low profile, not knowing the situation at St. Patrick's or if the police were looking for him at all.

After a few anxious moments, Peter stepped down out of the ambulance and turned. "You and *little Pete* will be fine," he said. "I will be praying for you both."

"Thank you for everything," she said. "I know we will… God

bless you!"

Peter closed the door and he and Sergetti watched the ambulance driver lay on his horn and speed away.

"Little Pete?"

Peter's face twisted into a grin. "She insisted," he confessed. "Besides, it is a good name, no?"

† † †

"If there was ever a sign, this has to be it," Elizabeth said, pun intended.

Paul just stood in silence, gaping at the marquee. "This is hardly a coincidence," he said with complete confidence.

Liz smiled. "No, it's definitely not… so let's go see if we can find out when the show starts?"

Paul stepped back on the curb and grabbed Elizabeth's arm. "That sounds good, but first you need to get out of the street—that ambulance is coming right this way."

To Paul's surprise, the front door of the theater was unlocked when he pulled on the handle. Inside, the lobby was dimly lit and smelled old. Creepy ornamental iron light fixtures with stained glass shades dangled from the high ceiling and were dimmed down to just enough light to see. The walls from floor to ceiling, from what they could tell, were mahogany, darkened with age, and a scarred Victorian chiffonier stood in the center of the room. Paul was the first to notice the movement from behind the desk.

"We're not open yet," a gravelly voice called out. The man barely looked up as he spoke.

"We're sorry to bother you, we were just wondering when the show starts?"

The man closed his book and managed a meager smile. He removed his readers and focused on Paul and Elizabeth. "The show is not for a few hours—" he said. He glanced at his watch and shook his wrist. "The doors open at six-thirty, but the show doesn't start until eight."

"Is it a comedy? A musical? What?"

"All of the above," he replied.

"And it's about Simon Peter?" Liz asked.

The man smiled and handed them both a flier. "Indeed it is."

Liz looked at Paul, her eyes sparkling.

"Thank you," Paul said.

"We're going to need to find a place to stay out of sight for a while," Liz whispered to Paul. "At least until dark…"

Overhearing the comment, the man came from behind the counter and slipped on a tattered, houndstooth jacket. "You people must be from the Sa-uth," he said with a loose imitation of a drawl.

"How did you ga-ess," Liz made an effort to smile. The man instantly reminded her of the professor.

"Well… I don't normally do this, but ah—we've got a room in the back if you need a place to stay until the show starts." His smile was warm and assuring.

Liz looked at Paul for guidance. "That would be great, thank you!"

The man fished a set of keys from his pocket and handed them to Paul. "It's right down the hall there," he said. "It's not much, but there's a couch and a coffee pot. Coffee and tea in the cabinet underneath. We use it for a break room, but the stagehands won't be in for at least another hour."

"You're very kind," Elizabeth said. Paul agreed.

EIGHTY-THREE
April 11, Saturday, P.M.

Yousef walked to the street corner and stopped. Standing a head taller than most, he scanned the street in both directions. He knew that one, if not all of them, had been there. He sensed it, as would a hound on the trail of a fresh scent. There was spiritual warfare going on here and he of all people knew it. For Yousef, a seasoned veteran of the highest demonic order, had been tasked with finding and eliminating the apostle, or at the very least disrupting his plans. But so far it hadn't happened and the thought of failing enraged him. And even though he didn't know why Peter had come to this particular place and time in history, he knew it had to be big.

Even his boss was clueless as to his true potential, because that's how he'd played it—for Mordecai to think he was in control when in fact he controlled nothing. Mordecai was a patsy, no more than a puppet in a high stakes game with eternal consequences, and he was completely oblivious. Yousef of course was privy to this. For centuries he'd wreaked havoc among God's children, but this was different.

The apostle had somehow transitioned through time and Yousef knew he couldn't. It was simply something they could not do and the whole situation troubled him. He had always been the one in control, empowered by a higher power. A dark power. An ominous power. But now he was worried. Was it all about to come to an end? Were the Scriptures about to be fulfilled? He shuddered at the thought.

† † †

"I have journeyed considerably farther today than the Sabbath would have allowed," Peter confessed, sporting a sheepish grin. He took the lead and the monsignor fell in behind, nodding at people like an insignificant passerby. To keep a low profile, Sergetti garnered a puffer jacket with a hood and removed his collar, but he was still uneasy and kept his head low. *No sense in tempting fate,* he thought.

Finally they came to the end of the street. "Seventh avenue and 46th," Sergetti read aloud. The numbers meant nothing to Peter, but the view certainly did. He pulled out the magazine photo and studied it for a moment. Then he held it out at arm's length and looked past it. Nothing. He looked at the photo again, hoping to catch something he hadn't seen before, something beyond the pixels and the blurred images that might give him a clue as to the secret he was looking for. But there was still nothing.

"What is it," Sergetti quizzed.

Peter wagged his head. "I thought—I thought I would find the answer here," he said. Folding the photo twice, he stuffed it in his pocket.

Sergetti scoped out the street. "Maybe it's something we're not seeing because it's not time to see it yet."

"What did you say?"

"Maybe it's not time to see it?"

"What is the t—time of day?

Sergetti pushed back his sleeve and examined his watch. "It is 6:18. Why?"

Peter looked directly at Sergetti, his eyes sparkling with

anticipation. "Because this is exactly where we need to be, it is just not the time yet."

EIGHTY-FOUR

April 11, Saturday, P.M.

"Can you believe this?" Liz asked, perusing the flyer. "The Big Fisherman right here in this theater! I mean, I'm just spit-balling here, but how could this be a coincidence?"

"It couldn't, Paul winked. "Now could I get a little more of that coffee if you don't mind?" He placed his cup on the table and Liz topped it off. For a moment she studied the carafe in her hand and her mood shifted. "Peter loves his coffee—" she said with a hint of remorse.

"We're going to find him Liz. I promise you. But I need to tell you something."

Elizabeth pulled out a chair across from Paul and sat down. "What is it?"

"When I called my wife she said someone from Mount Olive had called my house."

"What? What did she tell them?"

"She didn't tell them anything. She just said they would have to call back."

"That was smart."

"She's a pretty smart lady," he said. "But right now we need to find Peter, because I think when we do, all of this will make sense."

"I thought surely we would have found him by now," she said. "Maybe we should get back out there."

"Listen to me, this is where we're supposed to be right now," Paul insisted. "We're just around the corner from Times Square, which Peter said had great significance. And we've got a secluded place to lay low until we can figure out what to do. Just try to relax for a few minutes."

Liz managed a weak smile. She knew he was right.

"These are the famous Red Stairs," Sergetti explained. "This is where everyone comes when they visit the *Big Apple*."

Peter looked at him strangely. "New York," Sergetti corrected.

Peter nodded and took hold of the banister, pulling himself up to the first landing.

"Something is going to happen here tonight," Peter hinted. "In the ninth hour…"

"At nine tonight?" Sergetti asked.

Peter nodded guardedly, as if he was almost afraid to answer.

"But how do you know that?"

"I—I do not know how I know, I just do… at nine and eleven. These numbers have significance?"

Sergetti looked pleadingly at Peter. "Oh yes," he said. "9/11 was a day America will never forget. And it happened right here in this very city—at least part of it did."

Unexpectedly, two young women grabbed a seat next to Sergetti, chatting away and taking selfies. Sergetti motioned for Peter to follow him up a few rows. They found a space alone.

"God may have chosen this time because this number has great significance to all Americans," Peter went on.

Sergetti glanced over his shoulder then turned back to Peter.

"This could very well be an event the world will never forget," he suggested.

Peter agreed, sensing the gravity of the moment as the pieces of the proverbial puzzle seemed to be falling into place.

EIGHTY-FIVE

April 11, Saturday, P.M.

The room fell silent for a welcomed moment of respite. Paul was snoring when Elizabeth finally shut her eyes. They were both exhausted, physically and emotionally, and had been too wound up to sleep, but now, somehow they managed.

More than an hour had passed when Paul roused and slowly sat up. He stood with a wobble.

Liz stirred and dropped her legs over the edge of the couch. Her eyes swept the room.

"How long was I out?"

Paul strained to focus on his phone. "Over an hour."

"You're kidding me."

Paul rubbed his days-old beard. "You needed it though."

"I guess we both did," she said yawning. "I was dreaming…" she stood and arched her back.

"I was too…" he said. "More than one—what was yours about?"

"There were these huge screens and all of these people gathered in one place—" she described.

"You mean like Times Square?"

"Exactly like Times Square!"

"And the *Red Stairs*?"

"Yes the red stairs!" She said as their thoughts merged.

Paul grabbed his jacket and reached for the door. "Get your coat. It's time to go."

"So what was your other dream?" Liz asked.

Paul zipped up his jacket. "It's not relevant."

"Tell me."

"Fine, I dreamed I was sitting in church and I looked down and I was in my underwear. Happy?"

"Oh, I hate that dream," she said.

† † †

Darkness had descended on Times Square, and yet it seemed more vibrant and alive than the middle of the day. In keeping a low profile, Sergetti and Peter had moved again to another spot, one that felt a little more secluded, if there could be such a place on the infamous "Red Stairs."

"I am worried about my friends," Peter admitted. He fiddled with the bullet hole in his shirt. "Elizabeth, Paul and the professor. I wonder what has become of them?"

Sergetti perused the crowd. "I don't know what to say my friend. When I escaped they were being held at gunpoint. Then I heard the shot, but there was nothing I could do."

Peter touched Sergetti on the shoulder. "I know, I just hope they're alright."

"I do too," Sergetti said. "But what I failed to tell you was…" Sergetti stopped and glanced over his shoulder again. "The man was looking for you."

Peter recoiled. "For me? Why?" his voice noticeably rising.

"I don't know," Sergetti said.

Peter thought for a moment, then stood and walked the length of the long stair to the end. When he turned, he looked at Sergetti, then beyond. Tears sprang to his eyes as he scurried down the stairs to Paul and Elizabeth.

Eighty-Six

April 11, Saturday, P.M.

"I'm so glad you're safe!" Elizabeth cried, clinging desperately to Peter.

Sergetti joined the three and motioned for them to sit. *No sense in drawing any more attention than necessary,* he thought.

"And where is the professor?" Peter asked, not even considering what might have happened, but that was just Peter. Liz turned to Paul as if seeking his approval. She brought her hand to her chest and took a deep breath, regaining her composure.

"I'm sorry to have to tell you this, but the professor—was killed today Peter," she said, choking back tears.

Peter tightened his grip around Elizabeth's hand. "I feared something like this happened. I just did not want to believe it."

"I still can't," she said.

"I didn't know for sure what happened," Sergetti confessed. "I heard the gunshot, but I knew I had to get to Peter."

"There was nothing you could do," Liz said. "You took care of Peter and that's what was important."

"It's little consolation I'm afraid," said Sergetti.

"It was by God's grace that we were able to get out of there as well," Paul added. "And when we got back to the hotel we saw Mordecai and he was talking to Yousef. You remember Yousef, Peter?"

"From the garden… yes."

"Well it appears that he may have been the one who tried to kill Dr. Bernstein."

"Your friend in Israel?"

"The same. And apparently now he's connected to Mordecai."

Peter looked at Elizabeth in disbelief.

"So we decided to cut our ties with Mordecai."

"That was probably wise," Peter said.

"And that means we all have to be extremely careful," Elizabeth warned. "This situation with Mordecai and Yousef isn't going away. And if he did have something to do with David—with the attempted murder of Doctor Bernstein, he could do the same with—" she stopped and eyed Peter. "If something happened to you—" she said, shaking her head.

Peter thought for a moment and considered Elizabeth's theory. "What—kill me? But am I not already in heaven?" he asked curiously. "And have I not been there for two millennia?"

Elizabeth traded glances with Paul and Sergetti. She would have laughed had the situation not been so serious.

Peter shrugged and combed his fingers through his hair. "And yet I am here," he said.

"Indeed you are." Elizabeth gave a smile, but it quickly faded.

EiGHtY-8EVEN

April 11, Saturday, P.M.

Vehicle horns varying in pitch and decibel filled the air as the drone of combustion engines and squealing brakes painted the scene. As with most of the city, Times Square teemed not only with traffic, but also with droves of people crisscrossing the streets in every direction. Midway up the Red Stairs, Liz, Paul and Sergetti sat with Peter and watched.

"God has spoken to our brother Peter's heart—" Sergetti hinted. He turned to Peter. "I assume it's okay if I share this?"

Peter nodded consent.

Sergetti scanned the people around him for a moment before he went on. "He believes that something is going to happen here tonight… at 9:11 actually." He glanced at his watch.

Liz sat straight up. "Here in Times Square?

Peter nodded guardedly.

"I knew it! I've felt it in my bones ever since you tore that photograph out of the magazine. I even dreamed about it," she admitted. Peter seemed to appreciate the confirmation.

"What do you think is going to happen?" Paul asked flatly.

"I am not certain, but I am confident He is able…" Peter smiled as if he were privy to more than he was willing to share.

Paul glanced at his phone. It was 9:05. "Is there some place we should be, or—"

Peter looked into the night sky, as if seeking guidance. "No, this is where the Master has directed us."

Paul stood and skimmed the crowd one last time when out of the corner of his eye he caught sight of a brooding familiar face. He winced. Realizing he'd been made, Yousef bolted straight for them. Paul spun around just in time to witness the angel Manasseh materialize in front of Peter. Then in an instant, Yousef vanished into the crowd.

EiGHTY-EiGHT

April 11, Saturday, 9:11 P.M.

Something was different, and strangely so, as with an animal sensing an impending doom or the bristling of hair on the back of one's neck. Without warning, the wind stilled and the pressure changed, as if all the oxygen was being sucked out of the air. Then the Voice began. It was as if multiple voices spoke all at once in perfect unison and timbre—from the highest mezzo-soprano to the lowest basso-profundo and an infinite range of notes between. The words *'I AM'* bludgeoned the sound waves as every human being seemed to stop at once.

As the four watched in utter amazement an eerie stillness settled over the city that seemed to last for hours, though only seconds passed. In the quiet of the moment a gust of wind stirred loose paper in the street as the traffic snarled and slipped into a sort of suspended animation. People from every direction, from every bistro, theater and apartment building moved into the streets. Taxicabs and automobiles were suddenly abandoned as drivers and their patrons gravitated toward the massive screens that surrounded Times Square. But there was nothing on the screens, not in a visual sense, but those who truly sought to see did so—as if a spiritual telepathy guided them.

A child cried. A woman signed the crucifix on her chest. A drunk studied his bottle, then flung it to the gutter as the Voice began with a boisterous, albeit calming resonance. And not a soul uttered a word.

"I AM THE GOD OF YOUR FATHERS—THE GOD OF ABRAHAM, ISAAC AND JACOB..."

A deafening silence settled over the multitude like a fog. The only noticeable sounds were the sighs of the penitent, the sobs of the remorseful and a sprinkling of scoffs from the ignorant who seemed to hear nothing at all—as if they were not even part of the conversation. Even so, no one moved.

In the twinkling of an eye, every human being who had the cognizance to comprehend did so as every hearing device known to man instantly sparked with energy. Cellphones that hadn't worked in years gathering dust in junk drawers suddenly energized. Batteries were instantly charged to capacity. Phones that were well out of reach of cell towers began to ring. Even people with hearing aids and cochlear implants miraculously perceived each word with perfect acuity as the Voice continued.

"WHERE WERE YOU WHEN I LAID THE FOUNDATIONS OF THE EARTH? TELL ME IF YOU HAVE UNDERSTANDING..."

The strange, rhetorical question hung in the air for a moment, as if taunting anyone to respond, though no one did.

"WHO DETERMINED ITS DIMENSIONS AND STRETCHED OUT THE SURVEYING LINE? TO WHAT WERE ITS FOUNDATIONS FASTENED

OR WHO LAID ITS CORNERSTONE AS THE MORNING STARS SANG TOGETHER AND ALL THE ANGELS SHOUTED FOR JOY? SURELY YOU KNOW!"

The words, taken directly from the Scriptures, were admittedly divine though they were foreign to most. Some even perceived them as arrogant and condescending, but no one dared speak of it.

"NO, YOU DON'T KNOW, BECAUSE YOU LACK SPIRITUAL UNDERSTANDING. BUT I WILL TELL YOU OF THE THINGS I SEE, THINGS THIS ONCE GREAT NATION HAS BECOME. FOR I HAVE SURELY SEEN THE OPPRESSION OF MY PEOPLE AND IN THEIR SORROWS I HAVE HEARD THEIR CRIES...

YOU HAVE TAKEN PATHS I NEVER INTENDED FOR YOU TO TAKE... FOR YOU HAVE MURDERED MY CHILDREN BEFORE THEY COULD DRAW THEIR FIRST BREATH AND YOU DID SO FOR THE SAKE OF CONVENIENCE. YOU ARE LIKE THE OSTRICH WHO FLAPS HER WINGS GRANDLY AND LAYS HER EGGS ON TOP OF THE EARTH, ALLOWING THEM TO BE WARMED IN THE DUST. BUT SHE DOESN'T WORRY THAT A FOOT MIGHT CRUSH THEM OR A WILD ANIMAL DEVOUR THEM. SHE IS HARSH TOWARD HER YOUNG, AS IF THEY WERE NOT HER OWN AND SHE DOESN'T CARE IF THEY DIE. FOR I HAVE DEPRIVED HER OF WISDOM AND I HAVE GIVEN HER NO UNDERSTANDING..."

An uneasy silence followed, allowing the words to find their mark.

"YOU ARE MUCH LIKE THE OSTRICH, AMERICA. YOU HAVE TAKEN THE MEANING OF TOLERANCE TO HEIGHTS THEY WERE NEVER INTENDED TO GO. BY TAKING ME OUT OF YOUR SCHOOLS, YOU HAVE BOWED TO THE RAVINGS OF THE FEW OVER THE APPEALS OF MY CHILDREN. YOU HAVE DISGUISED LIBERTY AS NOTHING MORE THAN LICENSE, EVEN QUESTIONING MY PERFECT ORDER BY DECLARING THERE IS NEITHER MALE NOR FEMALE! LAODICEA HAS NOTHING ON YOU AMERICA. I WOULD SPEW YOU OUT OF MY MOUTH!"

There were no words to describe the gravity of the moment. There were those who raised their hands in praise and others who sank to their knees where they stood. There were those who bowed their heads while they stood and others who lay prostrate on sidewalks and in the streets without regard to anyone or anything around them.

Agnostics questioned their beliefs as atheists rehashed their philosophies. Theologians teetered as to the validity of the Voice and laymen praised as the Voice went on.

"AS IN THE DAYS OF NOAH, YOUR DAYS ARE NUMBERED AND YOUR TIME IS SHORT. BUT I AM A GRACIOUS GOD AND FOR THE SAKE OF THOSE WHO LOVE ME, I WILL AFFORD OPPORTUNITY TO ALL WHO ARE WILLING TO FOLLOW..."

IT IS FOR THIS REASON ALONE; I SEND TO YOU MY SERVANT, WHOM I HAVE GIVEN THE KEYS OF THE KINGDOM OF HEAVEN.

I GIVE YOU THE APOSTLE PETER."

EiGHTY-NiNE

April 11, Saturday, P.M..

There was a heavy, echoing silence that settled over the masses as the Voice vanished… but only for a moment. As quickly as it left, a bright halo of light appeared above the time travelers.

Again, the Voice boomed:

"I HAVE DIRECTED YOUR PATHS, AND I SEE YOU ARE STUNNED AND AFRAID. YET I WILL NOT LEAVE YOU WITHOUT SUCCOR. I HAVE PROMISED THE KEYS OF THE KINGDOM, AND THEY ARE BEFORE YOU. LOOK UPON THEM IN THE LIGHT."

The Voice, though directed at Peter, was also discerned by Paul, Elizabeth and Sergetti. But only them.

Then the light emanating from the cloud above shone down upon each one. A burst of lightning flashed and four bolts instantaneously shot down to them. Elizabeth shuddered when the burst touched the soft, underside of her forearm, instantly and painlessly inscribing the image of an ancient key in the flesh just above her wrist. Concurrently, those same symbols were emblazoned on the arms of Paul, Sergetti and Peter himself.

Again the Voice spoke to Peter.

"THEY WILL BE YOUR LIFE GUIDES... THE KEYS OF THE KINGDOM. THEIR WORDS AND ACTIONS WILL ULTIMATELY LEAD YOU ALL TO THE KINGDOM OF HEAVEN."

Then, as if on cue, the four took each other's hands and shared profound looks with a sudden, omniscient understanding of God's will.

As a gentle breath of wind swept the cloud away, they gazed over the silent crowd. There were now thousands upon thousands, and still no one spoke.

A moment passed and Paul whispered, "We have our answer." Behind the broad smile he swallowed hard. "We are the keys… and we are to be a part of Peter's quest.

With those words, the angel Manasseh transformed before all of them and the crowd separated as she led them down the stairs and into the square.

Yousef buried his head in his hands. He knew his time was short… and there was still much to do.

The End of the Beginning

What about you?

Has the Spirit of Christ spoken to you through these pages? Has there been a time in your life when you were ready to stop playing games with God like Professor Van Eaton? Why not today?

Romans 10:10, 13 For it is with your heart that you believe and are justified, and it is with your mouth that you confess and are saved. For, "Everyone who calls on the name of the Lord will be saved."

So it's up to you.

Revelation 3:20 says; "Here I am! I stand at the door and knock. If anyone hears My voice and opens the door, I will come in and eat with him, and he with Me."

So Jesus stands and waits for you to open the door to Him. And if you sincerely ask, He will come into your life. Are you ready to settle it right now? If so, it's as simple as asking.

Here's a suggested prayer: Lord Jesus, I know I am a sinner and do not deserve eternal life with you in heaven. But I believe you died and rose from the grave to purchase a place in heaven for me. Lord Jesus, come into my life. take control of my life, forgive my sins, and save me. I turn away from my sinful ways and place my trust in You for my salvation. Amen.

If this prayer is the sincere desire of your heart, look at what Jesus promises to those who believe in Him.

John 6:47 I tell you the truth, he who believes has everlasting life.

Welcome to God's family, for today is your spiritual birthday, a day you will always want to remember! Now seek out a Bible believing church.

And will you share your decision with us? We would love to hear from you! Please let us know at:

questforthenailprints@gmail.com

**This salvation outline is based on the Evangelism Explosion program.*

ACKNOWLEDGEMENTS

Writing a novel is certainly not a feat for the faint of heart… I've learned that it's an all-encompassing event, evolving from sleepless nights, constant re-writes while riding the highs and lows of an emotional rollercoaster that never seems to end, at least that's how I see it. And that process is virtually impossible to do so alone. That said, I offer my humble and heartfelt thanks to my editor Susan Drake Robertson. Wow! We did it didn't we? Thank you for your expertise and sheer tenacity in keeping me focused, as difficult as that was! You are a stellar editor and Peter's Quest is a better story because of you! Your additions were exactly what was needed to keep the story on track and in step with where I wanted it to go. You're the best!

And of course I want to thank all of the alpha readers who read through my early drafts and added your own ideas to the story, (and most of them actually were added). Thank you too!

Finally, to my wife Karen. This has certainly been an amazing adventure, not to mention that in the midst of it all, you were put on the kidney transplant list and by God's grace, within two years, you received a perfect kidney! God truly has blessed us! And God bless you Sam Elliot, for your donation of life!

"All things work together for good to them that love the Lord, who are called according to his purpose." Romans 8:28

. . . On the Via Dolorosa

Don Furr is a teacher, author, and CEO of Exhibit-A, Inc., a trade show exhibit company located in Arlington, Tennessee. Married for thirty-nine years to his wife, Karen, Don is the proud father of three children, grandfather to seven beautiful grandchildren and one great-grandchild. He is also an avid fixed-wing and helicopter pilot. But by far his true love lies with all facets of movies, play writing, and his novels.

Don has written several screenplays and produced many live productions of Judgment House through his church, First Baptist Church of Lakeland, Tennessee, introducing others to Christ through that ministry. Don continually searches for new ways to utilize his talents for Christ. His latest endeavor, *Peter's Quest*, is a culmination of thirteen years of writing, editing, rewriting, more editing (well, you get the picture), and it has been the most rewarding and emotional journey he has taken to date.

Feedback? We'd love to hear from you!
Nailprintspress.com
Donfurr.com